Six Years of Impertinent Behaviour

A Short Story Collection

A M Montes de Oca

The Reworkd Press
Charlotte 2013

First published by The Reworkd Press, October 2013
Copyright 2013 by Amanda Moody Montes de Oca

"Squash Blossoms" previously published in *Souvenirs of the Revolution* (2013) by The Reworkd Press. Used with permission.

"Singer" previously published in PublishED. Used with permission.

Cover design by Amanda Stanford

Moody Montes de Oca, Amanda
Souvenirs of the Revolution/Amanda Moody Montes de Oca – The Reworkd Press, Charlotte, NC, USA.

1 Mexican-Americans – Fiction 2. Mexican-American Diaspora – Fiction 3. Women – Mexico – Fiction 4. History – Mexico- Fiction

ISBN 978-0-9889220-0-6

Manufactured in the United States of America

Six Years of Impertinent Behaviour

A Short Story Collection

A M Montes de Oca

Table of Contents

Singer

Last night I dreamt of my mother. She stood at the window, waist-high in water, watching her Singer sewing machine drown in the currents.

"I can reach it," I shouted at her, jumping headlong into the swollen river.

"Why?" she asked, but in my dream state nothing was more important to me than that old machine. I pushed against the force of the water, my knees obscured by the dark, treacherous eddies. The Singer sat at the bottom of the window box beneath us, surrounded by a strangely calm patch of clear water. I reached for it, holding onto the window ledge for support, glancing back at her apathetic face. She was looking at the Singer, not me, and it filled me with an ominous foreboding.

"Just let it go," she called to me. "It's rubbish and it's lost. Why hold on to it?" I was thrown head first into the river, the Singer retreating farther and farther from my outstretched hand. The Singer was an antique long before it came to be with us. We lived alone on a farm my father had bought out of nostalgia, and having moved us there, fifteen miles from the nearest small town, left one day and did not return. Without his presence, my mother's demons slipped out one by one, feeding themselves ravenously in the dark corners of the gloomy house.

She saw herself reflected in my face, and enviously tried to see into my thoughts. The demons would whisper to her, "That's your body. That girl has stolen your spirit." There were days she wondered aloud who the old woman in the mirror was, and why was she in her bathroom? At night she would sit up at the old Singer, prodding cloth through its teeth, making bibs for babies she no longer burped, aprons for kitchens she did not enter. She strained her eyes to make frilly dresses patterned on the designs of her youth and dressed me in them against my will, already at the age of twelve too old for flounces of lace and ribbons, smocking collars and ruffled ankle socks.

She filled the farmhouse with ornate china cabinets populated by a chorus of sternly smiling cherubim, dolls houses four feet high which I wasn't to touch, Rococo salon furniture, Chippendale dressers, table runners, doilies, and a stencil kit to paint a menagerie about the staircases of frightening fantastical animals whose beady, unseeing eyes would follow me around the house. I wasn't to play in certain rooms, nor allow my friends from school to come over. "What do you need friends for?" she would ask bitterly. "They'll just leave you in the end. All you have is your family. No one will love you like your family does."

I never knew how she busied herself while I was away, except by the evidence of her ambition – the painted minions of strange beasts adorning the wooden panels who multiplied in my absence, the mountains of newborn baby layettes which she folded neatly into cedar chests and rusty filing cabinets.

Then as I grew, one by one the old antiques, having been polished until the brass beneath silver plate came through and lacquer dulled with the rubbing of too many dust mitts, slowly disappeared as the demons convinced her they were fakes, worthless, to be thrown into the compost heap like rotten food. They drifted there, bits and pieces of iron and ancient workings, like demented clocks made of splintered chaos, still ticking, until a neighbour couldn't stand it anymore and had the heap cleared away.

It wasn't until they had taken her to a state hospital and she withered there like a hot-house flower in an arctic garden that I learned how insidious the spectres of her mind really were; whispering, tormenting, accusing her of imagined crimes and imprisoning her intellect behind a veil of paranoia.

"Have you met my little girl?" she asked me once, just before she died.

"No," I replied, curious.

"She's a devious one; selfish, beautiful, cruel." My mother glanced over her shoulder and whispered furtively. "Is she in this room?"

"Yes," I said. "See just there? Look next to the window," I pointed to the mirror above her sink, "Go and see."

The Lame Lammmie's

Pajammies

When I was eight years old a lamb was born on our farm that was lame, but instead of sending it to the slaughter house, my mother decided she could teach it to walk herself.

The night it was born my father took hold of my foot until my eyes opened to the pitch black of our silent house.

"Get dressed and come out to the barn," he said. "But don't wake your brother. Put on your outside clothes – the ones that are already dirty."

I knew then that it would be good – Omar hated to be dirty, to smell of grass and hay, of the animals' sweat. Everything that was fun was dirty: wringing chicken's necks, cutting up worms and small fish, catching rabbits, digging in the bog. Omar stayed inside if he could and nosed his thumb at me when I came home late in the night smelling of my adventures with our father.

The barn was a small animal shed with a sheep trough, a chicken coop and a rabbit hutch, a space for grain, hay bales and a water faucet. In the winter, the tin walls howled and groaned with the strain of snow drifts and dark gales. When I pulled on my rubber boots and clomped through the snow to the barn, I saw that my father had hollowed out a small niche far from the door and holding pens. He had strewn hay and old quilts on the floor and hung tattered blankets on the walls to keep out the draft.

"Hunker down," he said quietly. "Sit on your heels. Don't move."

I made myself small beside the iron rails of the sheep pen and waited as my father and his dog led in the ewe. She kept to my father's side, away from his dog, her eyes wide and white, icicles in her shaggy wool that tinkled like bells.

"Heel, Buddy," my father said, and the dog hunkered down as I had done.

The ewe went to the corner, and smelling me there she knelt with her back to me. Her eyes only closed when she saw Buddy lay his head down on his paws as my father shut the pen. She panted, and her sides heaved.

My father slowly moved to join me, motioning for the dog to stay where he was.

"What's happening?" I whispered.

He put his finger to his lips. "Watch," he said. "We're only here to watch."

The ewe's back quivered as though to shoo flies, though I knew there could be none – we found them frozen against windows and old buckets, they did not survive the first snowfall. The ewe's warm breath billowed like puffy clouds and cigarette smoke and then, as I lost feeling in the backs of my knees, the ewe bleated and she stood up suddenly, dragging a large sac behind her.

"There," my father said quietly, pointing with his chin. "Wait. Don't stand yet. Don't move. There might be another."

The ewe bleated again and nudged the sac, a bundle of sticks and knobs; a white pile of disjointed doll parts. The ewe licked the lamb's nuzzle and nibbled away at the sac until the lamb's head was free and it feebly echoed her bleating. Once he did, the ewe lay back down and my father's body tensed with excitement. "Another one," he whispered.

The ewe stood again with another sack, but unlike the first, the second lamb stood immediately on wet shaky legs and wobbled toward his mother, nosing beneath her hanging belly, bunting it with a glistening head of perfectly white, kinked wool.

"Get up," my father whispered beside me. I turned to him, confused. He said it again. "Get up."

The first lamb, still a bundle of legs, limbs, and goo on the hay-strewn floor convulsed and strained but did not stand. My father sat up, impatient for the lamb to do the same, and when it did not, he paced nervously. The ewe nudged the first lamb with her nose as the second lamb nudged her belly. She bunted them both with her head, urging the first lamb as my father dared not do.

"Why won't it get up?" My mother spoke behind us in her strange voice, oblivious to our hushed anxiety, causing my father to curse.

"There's something not right with it," he said.

"Well. Go see," her voice was clipped in the thin, dry air.

He turned his back to her, angry beneath his veneer of calm. "All that," he said. "What a waste."

The ewe had taken the younger lamb to the far side of the pen, warily watching my father as he nudged the other lamb, still flailing his thin limbs and bleating feebly.

"It's lame," he announced to us. "Won't walk." He sighed and wiped the cold sweat from his brow. "I'll take it to the slaughter house in the morning."

"It needs to eat," proclaimed my mother, pulling her blue-black hair away from her face. "I go make a bottle."

"Gelus,"

But she had already turned to go back up the slippery path to the house.

My father groaned and noticed I was still there, still silent, waiting for the lamb to walk. "Can I see the other lamb?" I asked.

He nodded and I crawled between the iron grates to the mother and her baby, side stepping the wet piles in the dull brown hay.

"Careful you don't startle them."

I put out my hand to the ewe's panting muzzle, letting her smell the hay and grain dust on my fingers, the scent of the barn on my sweatpants, the deliberate calmness of my touch. She bleated and licked my salty fingers. The lamb she had pinned behind her became curious and ventured a peek at me. His eyes, black pools of liquid, searched me for milk, for food, for something useful. He sniffed me tentatively, the warm sponge of a nostril delicate on my skin. He did not smell like the dirty ewe, covered in melting ice – he smelt like musty clothes and the rusty odor of boiling blood.

"I have this," said my mother entering noisily, her voice startling the ewe, the lamb, and myself.

In her hands she held an eye dropper and a glass of milk.

"You can't feed it with that."

"Yes. I can feed it with this." She pulled her woolen trench coat about her more tightly. "I will not let this poor thing die," she said, her fierce black eyes defying my father to pit his farmer's wisdom against her saintly compassion.

"Gelus," he said, "that lamb cannot walk. It must go to the stock yard."

She began filling the eye dropper and tried to sit beside the sickly lamb without touching anything unnecessarily. "You are cruel," she said, a stress on the wrong part of the word. "You don't know it cannot walk."

"I do know it can't walk."

"I teach it," she said again, shrill as before, her round almond eyes flashing daggers, her pink cheeks hot house flowers in an arctic garden.

"Gelus, you don't know the first thing," he said before trailing off. "Even back in Mexico," he began to say. "They wouldn't,"

"This isn't Mexico, is it?" she pierced the air with her voice, her sharp teeth set in each word, "I left there to be with you, remember? This my house, my lamb, and I want to teach lamb to walk. Okay with you, Mister doctor of animals?" His shoulders slumped and he sighed. "Fine." He lifted me into his arms and out of the sheep's pen where my misty breath had hung on every barbed word. "Time for bed, little one," he set me on the path to the house. "And don't wake your brother."

"Hey." Omar shook me the next morning, rattling the wrought iron princess bed our mother had specially ordered. "Come see this."

He was dressed for the day in his favorite jeans jacket, matching cap and boots. I pulled on something from the floor and crawled after him, wiping my eyes and scratching my tummy. We crept down the wooden steps to the landing. Something smelt like spoiled food, animal poop and Lysol.

"What is it?" I whispered.

"Look," he said and pointed to a doorway.

There hung the lame lamb from a harness fixed to the ceiling, wearing one of my old footie pajamas with the feet cut away – purple fleece with white trim. The body suit fit him perfectly, the zipper lovingly snug and secure, a latch cut away from the lamb's back end.

"Weird, huh?"

I nodded.

Beside the lamb were six bottles of milk fashioned from old nipples and pint sized milk jugs, fresh towels stacked on top of our washing machine, and a new blanket covering the checkered linoleum floor.

The lamb dangled there serenely, a toddler on a swing, his head drooping as he slept.

Our mother bustled in, humming under her breath. "Wake up, lambie, I have some nice milk for you!" she said in Spanish, pushing us out of the way. She clucked and fussed over the purple pajamaed, crippled baby lamb and fed him gently from one of the bottles. The lamb suckled eagerly, and butting her arm for more he bleat lustily and his tail whipped the air behind him with obvious joy.

"There," our mother said. "He going to be fine."

We crept away stealthily, watching our mother with jealous eyes, our ears red and ringing with songs of which we had no memory of ever having heard before.

Magdalena

She had hard-working hands. A labourer's hands. Her mother had read her palms when she was a girl and said it would be a difficult life. "You will marry a good man, but he will always be poor," she had said.

Her mother was a diligent woman, who spoke only when was necessary. It was a childhood of cleaning stranger's clothes, the tolling of church bells and taxi horns marking the slow passage of time. After her mother's death, Magdalena and her husband left the country of her birth while she was still suckling her firstborn, a baby who did not cry. She had named it Maria for the Virgin, and said her last prayer when croup took the child from her breast during the harsh winter winds. She named the second baby Maria as well, but life was kind and the child lived.

Each day Magdalena boiled her husband's coffee and blessed him so he would find work, put on her many layers of thin woollens and a coat which looked like a beggar's quilt, and took Maria to school. Then, she sat down in her usual place to beg for alms, far from the noisy, mud-splattered and graffiti-stained tenement where she lived.

She was used to the Northerners, with their preachy, indifferent charity – asking if she would choose a pound coin or a tube of toothpaste; who laughed delightedly when she pointed to the toothpaste, as though she had passed some secret test. Magdalena knew the looks and sideways glances of those who tossed in pennies and small change to her paper cup; the rueful smiles and apologetic mutterings of those who so rarely gave her a pound coin.

And then one day, lumbering up the walk, came a woman so large each step seemed precarious. Pausing for breath in the dull light of an autumnal afternoon, the woman dropped a pound coin into Magdalena's cup and looked her full in the face. "Hello," the woman said with a strange accent, "How are you today?"

Magdalena had heard of such people, but had never met one.

"I am cold," she replied. "And my liver is hurting me."

The woman nodded and said, "Mine too. The doctors keep testing my blood, but do nothing else. Useless." She smirked at the familiar complaint, so like her own. These Northern doctors with their over-cautious approach, she often complained to her husband, would rather you suffered than find out your illness is something they could not cure.

"I say the same." Magdalena shrugged and pursed her lips, "I say, it hurts me here, doctor, and he say he see me in six months, maybe get better, do nothing." It was then that the infant the woman had been carrying inside her coat pushed out its tiny head and gave a mewling cry. The woman put her pinkie finger into its mouth to soothe it. "I know it's too cold to be out with such a small baby, but I wrapped her up warm and her hat's on. It will be all right, won't it? I just need to walk off some of this weight. It will be okay, won't it?" The anxiety in her voice was strong, her uncertainty palpable.

Magdalena's knees creaked as she stood, and leaned in toward the woman's baby, buried in the soft layers of the woman's thick, dark cashmere, the sweet smell of the baby's head enveloping her senses. She stroked its pale cheek and it sighed.

"She is beautiful, madam. Do not worry. A healthy mother have healthy baby. Is good you walk. Is good baby close to you." She patted the infant's cheek again before settling herself back onto the sidewalk, under the tartan blankets someone else had thrown away.

"Do you have children yourself?"

"Yes. A girl. Five years."

"What's her favourite dinner?"

"Roasted chicken. I make like my mother make."

"Well, that's easy enough," the woman said. "Hold on; I'll be right back." The woman tottered away and returned with a shopping bag. Inside was an entire chicken, a bag of lentils, five fresh oranges, dishwashing powder, and hand lotion. She waved, smiled, and was gone. The cold wind groaned and whipped down the alley way beside her, it rushed the river's water beneath her into swirling dark eddies. The stone bridge Magdalena sat upon, ancient and necessary, was silent and unyielding. She wondered if her own daughter would one day be like this woman, this stranger in an unfamiliar place. A bird called out. Magdalena glanced up into the greying afternoon sky to see a lone seagull, its white wings dipping into the river, rushing to a place she could not see.

Fish in a Doorway

They had been travelling for forty-five minutes before either spoke. It was the girl who broke their silence. "What's this one about again?"

The boy turned his face away, frustrated that he must repeat everything he said at least twice, frustrated that he need speak at all. "Something to do with fish. I don't know exactly."

The girl knew he was annoyed, but she asked him these questions because of his annoyance, not in spite of it. "What will they do with the fish?" she asked.

If he groaned or at least rolled his eyes she would have won. This made the girl remember something funny from the past and she laughed, but quickly silenced herself. She glanced over at him, but knew he wouldn't want to hear the story. The boy didn't like to hear about the past.

"I don't know what they'll do with the fish. You know I don't."

They travelled another thirty-five minutes and then the boy stood. The metal doors of the train opened and the girl followed him out onto the platform. They began walking. The streets and wooden houses were deserted; they found the festival by its noise.

There, by the sea, were four fish. Two were red and two were black. They were as large as ships with wooden frames pulled tight by canvas skins; their scales glittered in the sunlight. She felt sorry for the huge wooden fish, lifted high by thirty men each, out of the water and choking.

The boy took out his camera and began to look for a good place to stand in the crowd. The men lounged on the dead withered grass of July, seeking shade beneath the belly of their fish.

Then, a cry rose up from near the red fish on their far left. It was lifted high from beneath its beams of cedar and lunged forward. In a circle the men carried the red fish, close to the crowd that had gathered round. As the men passed them the boy snapped photos and the girl stared into the fish's bulging eye. The men holding the fish began to run. Their lungs burst with Asahi breath and cheap cigarette smoke as they shouted, chanted, and finally smashed the fish face first into a doorway.

The crowd cheered; children atop shoulders, wives leaning on husbands, they roared as the men pulled the fish from the *tori*. Its face had caved inside itself and the eye had collapsed and now hung downward. It looked at the crowd reproachfully, sadly, as the men lay the broken fish upon its resting place by the shores of the dull brown sea. The men clasped each other fraternally, readjusted *yukatas* and torn sandal straps, found fresh beer cans and lit new cigarettes.

Then came the black fish, the red fish, the black fish and then the crowd dispersed cheerfully to inspect the *tori's* damage, to see what was left of the beautiful wooden fish.

The people touched the torn canvas, the splintered wood; they let their children play on the carnage. The boy walked slightly ahead of the girl, and stopped three paces from the first red fish to photograph the children who played on the beams. He smiled as they waved to him and called to him in a language he didn't speak.

She wanted to be as serene as he was, or as excited in their good luck in finding this obscure place and it's strange rituals — to love and find them fascinating, or if only, to find speaking as unnecessary as he did. But even as the children played, the girl saw the dying fish had acquired ghastly grins, appeasing, and they were mutilated.

"Where did you find out about this?" the girl asked the boy, but he didn't bother to reply. He had finished photographing the children and began to wander down to the shore. The boy put his hands on his back and stretched. He shielded his eyes to scan the fishing boats and empty nets, and looked towards the land at the end of the sea.

Soon the boy returned from the edge of the sea and the girl followed him back to the train station. They waited for eight minutes and then boarded the train. The boy and girl sat down and as the train rocked on its rails the girl was lulled to sleep on the boy's shoulder.

The Back Room

It is early on a Monday morning and not many people are in the terminal of Benito Juarez International Airport in Mexico City. The police officer spots me as my bag goes though the X-ray. He strolls over casually and looks me up and down, as if sizing up my ability to pay, squirm away, or cause problems. I look back at him with my practiced stare (that stare designed to look like everyone else.)

"*Es tu bolsa*?" he asks menacingly.

"Yes," I say, definitively with the lilt of a question – and I answer in Spanish, "It is my bag."

"Please follow me," he says. He wears no name badge, and I consider running away for a split second.

We go in the back room. I have been in several back rooms; Egyptian ones, Japanese ones, British ones. But this was Mexico – where I was born. Often, I joke about the Mexican back room because I know: these were my people. Here, I do not know just a few phrases about the price of beer and please, where is the bathroom - I can translate humor, argue literary points, and explain subtle nuances of political policy. I do not belong in the Mexican back room.

It is small, cramped, and isolated. The door closes but not completely—there is a bend in it where the damp air has warped the wood. The people milling about outside make an effort to turn their backs (though I am visible through the crack) as if to say to everyone else: Move along, nothing to see here.

The officer dumps out the contents of my backpack. He opens the various makeup bags stuffed full of silver and dumps them out too. "You have receipts?" he asks me.

"No," I explain, "It was the *tee-an-ga-wees*," deliberately mispronouncing the word so as to make it seem as though I am not Mexican at all—simply a confused and hapless tourist. Though this usually works with non-Americans, I do not realize it is the wrong tact to take with this particular officer—brown, native, perhaps he lives in some slum outside the airport, perhaps he hates that I am leaving, and that he must stay behind.

"Hm, this is a problem," he muses, shifting through the earrings, bracelets, rings, and necklaces. He holds one up to inspect it. "This is some fine stuff here."

I bring water to my eyes and say pitifully, "But no one told me. My cousin is a Federal officer also, and even he did not tell me." Neither the crying nor the name dropping work—the officer is used to tears (having probably caused them many times), and Mexico City is a long way from Puebla.

"Don't cry," he says, and it's a command.

I stop crying and nod my head; I look down at my hiking boots, thinking fast. "Maybe there is a fine I can pay?" I ask.

He considers this. "I'll be right back," he says, tossing bits of silver back onto the table with my backpack. He leaves the room and paces the hallway, speaking on his cell phone. He also turns his back to me. I pray silently, "pleasegodjustletmegopleasegodjustletmego."

The officer comes back, adjusts his automatic machine gun at his side, and crosses his arms sternly. From his great height he looks down at me; I brace myself for a lecture. "This is a problem, my supervisor agrees," he says quietly and pauses. "You tell me what we're going to do. What are we going to do?" He leans toward me and I look into his eyes: they are as black as mine. I look at his clean cut face, his brown leather skin—oiled and unlined—his perfectly cut hair, the color of a raven; the same color as my mother's before hers turned grey.

For only one moment I don't know what he wants. In that moment I forget myself. My thoughts float, nebulous, my synapses cannot connect—they only see the machine gun strapped to his side, his polished boots, his bottomless pupils—and then my mind sees the magician behind the curtain. The officer wants a bribe.

I quickly take out my wallet and hand him all the cash inside (300 pesos, about 30 US dollars). He motions to the coin purse in my other hand but I snap it open to show him—it's empty and in spite of everything, I want smirk at his disappointed expression. He points to my old Minolta. I only pause for one millisecond before nodding (I have another Minolta and two Pentax at home). He takes my camera and opens his jacket, nestling it inside the voluminous padding, watching my reaction at the same time. I make no reaction—I know better than that. The only thing I regret him taking is the vintage strap; I found it in Osaka after a lengthy search.

He puts his finger to his lips as though we are conspirators together, playing spy and secret agent, and still holding this ridiculous pose, he opens the door to let me out.

I walk past the Duty Free shops full of Lancôme make up, Lacoste tee-shirts and Starbucks cappuccinos to the electric walk way that leads to the terminals.

My chin is quivering. I feel very small.

Talisman

"That's a study talisman, Lizzie's got one on her schoolbag," Kenny said, so I put it back.

The old Japanese woman smiled at him, thinking he was guiding me, that no one could choose a talisman without help. She gestured to them, the many rows under the temple's wooden awning. Some were blue, or pink or purple or white or green, all embroidered with gold thread and Kanji, neat stacks of talismans in drawers like silverware. They seemed so small, insufficient bits of fabric encased in plastic.

"Here's one for drivers, one for salary men," he said pointing, careful not to touch. "To get married, to be fertile, to protect children," he continued through the stacks, as if I wanted one, a souvenir of this island temple of tall trees.

"I don't want one," I said, thinking of Lizzie's mischievous eyes and quick fingers, her Pokemon and Battle Beetle playing cards, how she tried to get me to take her to the Shrine during our lessons. "Not one that says it can guarantee study, or marriage. And especially not one that says it will protect children." I should be able to do all that myself, I thought.

"I wish we could buy Lizzie this one," he said quietly, musing, "put it round her neck like a tag, 'Evil stay away'." He bit his lips and folded his arms around my shoulders.

Who will be Lizzie's talisman, I wondered, when we have all gone home?

Our school is startlingly still at six thirty. The stairs are dark with night; no one leaves the lights on. The other teachers forget about Kenny and me; that we stay until eight. In their eagerness to be rid of the kids and mess, lights are shut off and doors closed. Sometimes even my night students forget about me- Junior High kids too busy with their endless exams to show up for an ESL conversation class. The five-story building is silent then, waiting for the next day. My slippers slide across wood floors with no sound.

That was usually when Lizzie came down to the school. Sometimes she smelt of her dinner, fish sticks and sticky rice balls. Sometimes she smelt of urine and dirt, a week's unbathed filth on a three year old's body. And sometimes she smelt of her father.

"Miss Manda," she'd sing, an A swallowed by an M, and I'd occupy her with some craft so I could finish my planning. The kitchen we worked in was so still we sometimes whispered, our foreheads touching.

"What did you do today?"

Now sticky fingers turning my head, a rush of breath in my ear, fish breath. "After Miss Manda's class went to Grandma's."

"Did you play with Grandma?"

Her nose wrinkles. "Silly Miss Manda. Grandma too old! What's this?" Lizzie would then ask, listening closely with a half-opened mouth, staring into my eyes while I explained.

"It makes big circles, look." I draw one on her paper.

"You need it?" She struggled with the protractor to copy my circle.

"Not really, Lizzie Ann-chan," I'd say. "You can use it."

Some nights she didn't come down until almost eight, and then nearly always smelt of her father.

"Read me a story," Lizzie would say flatly as she pulled random books from the bookshelf and crawled into my lap on the scratchy sofa.

"Why don't you read me one, and then I'll read you one?" I'd ask gently, stroking her hair. I knew she wanted me more than the books, that I hold her like a baby, as if she were mine. Some nights she would refuse everything and crying with frustration, stamp her feet, one sock missing. Not a baby but an angry little girl, exhausted by sleepless nights. I would pull out the special big box of crayons and the special big paper. Paper and crayons were Lizzie's world. Her pictures were always bright, usually in pink.

"This is the School," she'd say, pacified by the paper and the voice it gave her, a baby pointing to a sectioned box. "And this is my house," again pointing to the box, but higher up. "Down, School, up Lizzie's house." Sitting back and sliding a finger along a dividing line, "This is where mommy sleeps, and this is where daddy sleeps." Biting a crayon, saliva stuck to blue, she points to another box. "Here is Lizzie." Mumbling now, indistinctly, the words of someone else, "Lizzie. Lizzie is a princess."

We stared at the rows of talismans again, the evil they promised to guard against, the prizes they could grant. The cedar trees of the island rustled and shifted the sunlight; spread their scent past the Temple, the round-bellied Tanuki's, and the fierce lions. A woman clapped in front of the Temple and gave a swift bow to the ancestors behind the steel and wooden grates. We linked hands and watched her, hoping for a secret, a word, something to transcend a talisman, something for a little girl who sometimes smelt of fish sticks.

The Hotel Evaluator

The woman in front of Nathan Wilson was having a bad day. For starters, she was overweight, and being so, had sweat through her t-shirt in the ninety-five degree heat. Also, it was one o'clock. So at that moment, sweaty from driving and late for lunch, the woman in front Nathan Wilson in the lobby cafeteria was only interested in one thing—cutting ahead in line.

"But I'm not ordering!" She insistently told the woman placing orders, "I'm having my food *a la carte*!"

Nathan Wilson glanced around the woman's girth at the food slowly coagulating under rusty heat lamps. He was only allowed to expense the buffet, but the rust concerned him. It was however, a buffet, not as the ravenous woman mistakenly and fancily over-frenchified it, an *a la carte*.

"I only want a salad," she insisted again. The others before them viewed the buffet choices with as much suspicion as he did and rather chose to order lengthy dishes—minusing this and adding that—taking up more valuable time which could otherwise be spent inhaling lettuce and shredded carrots. Inch by inch the buffet was finally and successfully reached. However, the white wine was now gone. Incensed and at her final reserves, the portentous lady puffed out her chest and enquired in a deep alto, "Are you the...Hotel Manager?"

"Yes, ma'am. I'm sorry we're out of..."

"Well," the woman interrupted, so inflated she resembled a stuffed puffin, "If you are the...Hotel Manager...we have another matter to discuss." She pointed a stubby finger threateningly.

"That woman," she began, loudly enough to be heard above the clattering by at least a five-foot radius, "told me I had to wait—whereas in your other establishments I am always allowed to go forward as I only ever get a salad." The rotund lady self-importantly finished with the shrill accusation, "But I knew! I knew I could go forward—I told her so. They always let me do so."

Nathan Wilson watched passively as the kindly manager apologized profusely to the woman, and as she passed, barely loud enough for anyone to hear he muttered, "You'd think she was the Hotel Evaluator!" With a chuckle he asked for coffee, black, and turned his back to the awful woman who had for at least six full minutes made him appreciate his loveless life and unbearable job—for at least he could say he had never quivered in righteous indignation at the tardiness of a tepid, limp and completely unappetizing buffet salad.

"You're the Hotel Evaluator?"

"Yes," he sighed as the peace the horrid woman's tirade had brought him quickly dissipated, "yes, I am."

"Oh, my. We hadn't expected someone so..." the possibilities: neat, nervous, gangly, thin, and frail ran through her mind, "tall. Please, come with me."

Nathan Wilson clutched his mug and followed the matronly manager down the hallway away from the lobby, knowing she was going to lead him a show room and try to convince him that the showroom was in fact, an operating standard guest room; as if he were a blind biddy who could not see the day-old spackle, the smell of newly unwrapped fabric and strong disinfectant. He used to argue with the managers when they did these things. Nathan Wilson would rant about the integrity of his unbiased opinion; insist that he didn't work for the company, no—he worked for the nameless consumer! But that was far behind him now.

Nathan Wilson did not bother the kindly manager with the fact that he already finished his report on the standard guest room and having been bored earlier two nights ago, also finished his reports on the other rooms the hotel offered. He did not tell her that the first morning as a guest, chatting contentedly about her children in Yugoslavia, being cheated at the money exchange and the price of gas, Nathan Wilson followed the leaning woman from floor to floor and had seen the entire hotel from behind closed doors—he knew every hotel's secrets.

Nathan Wilson instead did her the kindness of pretending to listen and politely smiled along as she explained the hotel policies and latest refurbishments, but his mind lay elsewhere.

It was Nathan Wilson's closely guarded secret that he found order frightening, patterns nightmarish—sameness ground his senses into a million pieces. He pretended to adore the sparseness of the showroom, lined with Escher drawings and geometric shapes, but his mind screamed in terror as he stood and filled out mindless reports in triplicate. And though Nathan Wilson stood perfectly still and gave no outward sign, his toes itched inside his shoes to be rid of that hellish regularity, that urbane normality and the steady metronome tick of the clock above the showroom door.

For in truth, Nathan Wilson hated his job. This should come as no surprise: a great many people hate their jobs. In fact, hating your job seems to be a rite of passage into the bitter hardships of Adulthood. So, while it wasn't surprising that Nathan Wilson hated his job, it was surprising how everyone else tried to talk him out of hating his job.

"But you're a Hotel Evaluator!" They would cry, "You're so lucky!" And though Nathan Wilson knew he was not alone in hating his job, he was alone—and extremely irritated—to find that everyone else thought his job was the greatest job on Earth. No one believed him that Hotel Evaluating was every bit as mundane as their own jobs - surely his was more exciting.

"But I'm an accountant, credit analyst, insurance underwriter," they would cry, "You're a Hotel Evaluator!"

It didn't matter that Nathan Wilson would explain the boring intricacies of forms filled out on paper, spreadsheet and word documents—the same information replicated in triplicate. Or that being in flight 52 hours each month was endlessly tedious. Or that most of the hotels he saw were chains and exactly the same in every city. Still they bleated like sheep round the trough, "But you're a Hotel Evaluator!"

Such people were annoying, exasperating even, but the true source of Nathan's anxiety was that he harbored a secret that could end his career in hotel evaluating and ruin his chances of making anything of himself in the hotel industry for Nathan Wilson was, tragically, color blind. His job—part of it, at least—was to look at simple repetitive décor and describe it eloquently, to transfer information from his eye to the page, images into words. He was meant to describe the playful display of color and light upon the artistically arraigned furniture and decorative yet functional amenities. He was encouraged to make the description "zing" and "pop". Nathan Wilson could not produce any of these sensations when he looked at a hotel. The company, in so many words, frowned upon Hotel Evaluators who could not perform this simple task, and so Nathan Wilson did the only thing he could. He made up another hotel and described that one instead.

Nathan Wilson did not lie about the hotel's structural condition or the upkeep of its various amenities. That information he reported faithfully in spreadsheets. He merely imagined another hotel entirely when writing its description in the word documents—and no one ever realized that hotels he had described as Art Deco were in fact Art Nuevo and that hotels decorated in earth tones were described as "blues and soft reds provincially bathed in natural light."

And so, alone in his hatred of his job, unable to accurately describe cookie-cutter chain hotels, Nathan Wilson punished himself viciously. He researched the worst hotels his company offered. He rated them and on his own time Nathan Wilson reviewed them in a personal file, kept on a personal data stick—never to be seen by anyone else.

When he described those hotels Nathan Wilson did not lie, for he seldom wrote of their color schemes or décor. For color schemes, most of these hotels mixed water and last years' left over paint, and décor was bought at salvage shops and supermarkets. Nathan Wilson would trudge through back alleys and four lane highways, ride the subway deep into the wrong end of town, take abuse in several languages and work 12-hour days—all in punishment for his inability to fabricate eloquent market-speak descriptions of the better hotel chains.

Gradually, Nathan Wilson began to be proud of his efforts and the time he spent in gathering and correcting misinformation in the honest descriptions he provided. He began to read them to himself before bed, making of them a personal catalogue of bedtime stories to bolster his confidence.

Guests visiting the Riviera Hotel on Sommerset Avenue will be delighted by the cool ocean breeze the kicked down doors afford on summer nights. The charming "street smart" décor and bullet holes offset the damaged fixtures and cigarette-burnt sheets. Guests wishing to freshen up will find the gaping hole in the side of the building's main lobby particularly accessible to the pool area.

And:

The Weather-All Hotel has recently discovered air-fresheners in time for mold season. Guests will enjoy the influenza left by previous guests and delight in the hilarious surly retorts of the impatient and rude desk staff.

However, he lay in his bed troubled on this night, for the hotel he had witnessed the day before shocked even Nathan Wilson, who had seen thousands of hotels. He had seen missing walls, rats, vermin, and vagrant live-in guests. He had his personal litany of the 5 Signs of a Budget Hotel—but this; this was quite another thing entirely.

His company described the hotel in question thus:

This historic hotel in downtown Detroit offers complimentary parking and laundry service for a small fee. Local calls are complimentary and a wireless Internet access permeates the lobby.

Nathan Wilson had described it thus:

Guests may enjoy the dangerous atmosphere of this historic downtown Detroit hotel. Sirens screech into the night as police arrest yet another porn kingpin. Should guests move aside the torn, dust-laden curtains and listen for footsteps they may hear it—as a wireless signal penetrates the hotel—a rumbling in the distance. Could it be? Yes, beneath the sound of stranger's fading footsteps and the clicking of hooker's high heels, destiny awaits.

While he was, he admitted to himself, actually frightened of hotel discussed in his imaginary description, it was not, unfortunately, an imaginary hotel. It was a disaster area; a brothel complete with pimps and ho's. That ignorant customers, mislead by the company's description, would chance upon a night spent in this stagnant cesspool of immorality deeply concerned Nathan Wilson. Their customers were families! They were unsuspecting honeymooners, under-funded students and people from Florida.

The manager he had spoken to on the telephone had not bothered to ask his name or business, but simply gave him the hourly rates and hung up the telephone. Nathan Wilson drove by it cautiously, lifting his aviator sunglasses to get a full look at its slum-glory. Inside he enquired about the advertised complimentary breakfast—it was a day-old doughnut from the convenience store next door, the prepubescent desk clerk informed him. The coffee was not complimentary, only the doughnut, an old man in tatters reminded the boy. Yes, yes, only the doughnut. The dour faced manager glared threateningly from behind bulletproof glass wallpapered with advertisements for bail attorneys and naughty nurse phone numbers.

And so it was that Nathan Wilson, back in his chain-hotel, contemplating his laptop in the middle of the night, began composing an email to his supervisors. He spent several moments thinking and fantasizing, knowing it would have to be a good email—worthy of the popular notion of a Hotel Evaluator. And as he knew no one had any inkling of what he did, that his work was shrouded in mystery and misinformation, this email would expose his most vulnerable point: his invisibility.

This was what he had thus far:

Hello,

I came upon this hotel as I was rewriting the region and have grave concerns. I know this hotel was not assigned for evaluation but I took it upon myself to investigate. Apparently, there have been reports by our customers that at this hotel you can either: rent a room by the hour and witness people who may or may not be a part of "the oldest profession" in the lobby. Several of our customers have complained to the board of health for a possible condemnation of the building. When I called the hotel, the desk clerk offered me a room for the hour based on the nightly rate. These issues concern me as we advertise this hotel on our service and if it is not a reputable establishment I would recommend we desist from representing it....

It was an email that was long in coming. Nathan Wilson knew at some point he would come across a hotel so rancid, so decrepit and irredeemable that even he dared not keep it secret. His ethical sensibilities demanded he send this email, and so, he was drowning those sensibilities with Sam Adams Boston Lager because he knew should he send it, even this small bit, he would receive an answer thus in reply:

Mr. Wilson,

We reviewed the hotel and your concerns. However, this is best left to a supervisor, as we have a tentative relationship with our hoteliers and need to be sensitive about the communication that comes from our service providers. In the future, please speak with your immediate supervisor so as he can advise the best course of action. He is acclimated to dealing with these types of concerns and can usually recommend or provide advice best suited to the particular hotel and market. Also, we will no longer be needing your services in the least. You're fired, you indolent and

unimportant fool.

Signed,

The Corporation

Because the truth of it was this: If anything were to transpire, it would transpire solely on the evidence of his confession. No one knew that Nathan Wilson privately visited roach motels. Those files were not trusted to the company laptop's hard drive. Even those reputable chain-hotels he did file, as part of his job description, did not merit his concern for they languished in shared folders into which no one ventured, or gathered dust on a continuously morphing supervisor's desk. His reports were squirreled away by whatever secretary had lost that week's pool. Entire months Nathan Wilson hid in his office altogether, unable and unwilling to meet one more boss, or shake another hand he knew would only vanish as quickly as it arrived.

But then at once, as though hearing a distant rumble of his own, Nathan Wilson hit the delete key several times and dug in his pocket for his personal memory stick. He could restore the files to their rightful places as factual representations of the hotels themselves! Nathan Wilson would neither have to expose or explain himself by email or triplicate forms. The act would signify all—and the entire Internet community and his loyal customer base would receive the reward of his personal punishments. Excited and clumsy, he loaded his files into the laptop and connected to the company's network. Certainly, their customers would read his descriptions before anyone at Corporate knew there was anything so tragically amiss. He might even take his overdue vacation weeks in the interim period; Nathan Wilson had always wanted to vacation in the Caribbean. The descriptions loaded within five minutes and within ten, Nathan Wilson was sleeping more contentedly than he had in years, and dreamt of monochromatic beaches, native-style huts and complimentary strawberry daiquiris.

Climbing Mt. Sinai

The trail at the base is very long and I walk by the light of a full moon. It is bright, but at the base there is nothing to look at but men bartering the use of their camels. I see others with jackets and hats. I only wear a sweatshirt. "Take a camel, Miss? Only forty Egyptian pounds." I shiver.

The bus down from Cairo took a long time, most of which I didn't remember but for the rocky, red landscape of the Sinai. The heat, the swaying motion, the soft seats always put me to sleep, and though I can sleep anywhere my favorite are the buses. We were on the only road, no other way across the desert and no structures within 50 miles. The bus stopped outside Sharm-el – Shek. The air was palpable but salty, unlike Cairo where the heat tasted like sand and smog. The people who left in taxis went to hotels and spas but the backpackers among us knew that Sharm was for old people, marrieds or tourists. *We* went to Dahab where the best part of the village faced the Red Sea. There, whitewashed hostels surrounded by tall skinny palms and shrubbery meet a long boardwalk and covered tents on the sand. We chose our hostel because its tent was covered in the brightest fabric walls and held down by elaborately painted poles – that and we saw a friend from Cairo there, Khaled.

"Ma'salama," he said, holding out fresh cigarettes.

"I'm going to climb Mount Sinai," I told him as I plunked down beside him.

"Long way up," he said, exhaling into the wind. I shrugged.

No one else wanted to come so I climb alone. The mountain is dusty, the rocks worn by countless pilgrim feet. I climb for two hours in a long upwards spiral. The path, well-worn and deserted is peaceful. But then the trail becomes narrow and steep and I begin to sweat and shiver in the night air. People on camels pass by and I begin to resent them. After three hours I stop by the side of the trail and sit down on the rocky ledge. I look down and see Dahab in the distance by the sea. Lights are blinking and I don't want to get up. I have a cramp in my leg and from months of smoking I can't catch my breath. My lungs are filled with crystalline razors. I shiver and watch people. A grandmother passes me, her face a map of criss-crossed roads. A Columbia brand hiking boot with red and gold laces plants itself in the dirt. Wearily, I look up.

"Hello there," a French accent, held between the teeth, greets me.

I grunt and the girl sits down to watch the people pass and lights of Dahab.

"Ready?"

I sigh and stand up. She wears a determined look – I guess she knows I would rather just sit on this cold desert mountain. We walk for five minutes when I hear a man speaking to me. "Camel, Miss?" I excuse myself from the French girl and agree. The man taps the camel's flanks and the huge beast roars compliantly and kneels. I climb on top of the animal and he lumbers up. Suddenly I am ten feet above the ground. I can see how narrow the path has become and I look over his head to see the bottom of the mountain; far, far down.

"Hold on, Miss," the man says. I take the camel's reins tightly and we start moving. Familiar with their lumbering gate, their gliding strides on cushioned hooves, I am not afraid of the camel. I am afraid of falling. I look up at the stars above the Sinai, hundreds upon hundreds of billions of stars that glitter like a bed of diamond dust.

We reach the first station of three. I get off the camel and the man turns to bring others. I sit and after a time I see the French girl. We continue up the mountain together. I begin to pant. The path is narrower and here there are no more camels. We pass the next station without stopping and suddenly we are at the base of a set of rock-cut stairs. I sit down on the first step, panting, sweating, with no will to climb up this solitary mountain where the grandmothers have more faith and stamina in their small toe than I do at all. The gentle breeze at the base of the mountain has turned into icy fingers that rake my face. There is dust in my throat. *I am a failure; I want to go home.*

"You are American?" the French girl asks. "Yes."

She nods, "My father was an American," she says quietly.

I nod also and agree – but I still am not moving myself up this staircase at the top of a mountain – holy or not. *Failure.*

"The sun will be up soon," she says.

I also agree with this.

"It would be a shame to miss the sunrise from the summit of Mt. Sinai on Easter morning."

I sigh and wipe my face with a dirty sleeve. I put my hands on my hips and look up to where the stars are still pulsing down at me. *Failure.* We stand and start to mount the large stone steps. Twenty minutes go by and I stop counting at eighty-seven, staring at my tennis shoes. The girl chats to herself in French, English and Swiss. She doesn't seem to notice or mind that I don't answer her. After an hour and a half we reach a plateau. There is the last station, a large shack that sells hot chocolates, religious trinkets and blankets. There are benches and I fall asleep on one. A second later I am shaken awake.

"I don't want you to miss it," the French girl hands me a blanket. *She bought me a blanket?* "The sun comes soon. There is one more set of steps to climb and then," her eyes mirror the stars above her, "we'll be at the top."

I hate the French girl.

I pull myself off the bench and wrap the blanket around me. My mind is numb and I can't feel my limbs. We join the line of pilgrims climbing the last steps to the summit. It isn't very high – only about twelve feet or so – and then among the large boulders at the top I find a place to sit down. I dangle my legs at the edge of the precipice and wrap the blanket around myself tightly. Far below me lie the foothills of Mt. Sinai and farther away, the dunes of the desert hills. They look like crumpled construction paper, lengthened shadows of moon and star light. I don't see the French girl and though I should be grateful to her, I am not. With my head on my knees, facing Israel at the summit of Mt. Sinai, again I sleep.

"Oooh, ahhh," the people say and I awake to see a pinprick of light in the distance. There, crowning the foothills is the sun. It grows until it blinds me, it grows until it touches the desert sands which sparkle like the stars had done, like the French girl's eyes had done and then it is day.

I turn and ask someone to take my picture. "Must we go back down the same way?" I ask the woman as she hands back my camera. "Oh, no," she says and her eyebrows arch at my poor Arabic. "There are steps that go down the entire length of the mountain side. They stop at Saint Catherine's monetary."

"How many are there?"

"Over a thousand."

I hang my head. We start down the mountain.

Four Strong Winds

These are the vast wastelands of west Texas. Parents who hope their children might go to the nearby junior college, toddlers speckled with dirt and raw blistered bug bites, young teenagers desperately searching the deserted avenue from the orange booths of the local gas station. In the morning Pack-A-Sack, meeting place for the 435 people of the town, doubling as the one convenience store/gas station within 15 miles of the next dirty town, is an anthill of gossip and a cloud of smoke. The old crowd comes in the morning, bringing with them news of impending babies, stained coffee cups, and a trail of Basic cigarette smoke. At night the young high-schoolers will chain smoke Marlboroughs, read tabloid horoscopes and tell each other how much they hate their parents, the authorities, school, the town itself. Conversations will linger on t.v., dating, and cars, but mostly gossip about who was not at the Pack-A-Sack.

I took myself out the door of Deliverance Grocery Store and let my mom smile and nod at the customer without me. I wandered outside into the suffocating heat of the dusty street. The man in the white truck gave me two seconds of his open palm, saying hello. Inside, old fattened hips dug into the counter-top as she leaned toward my mom, smushing her stomach so that it was forced to bulge under her t-shirt. "World's Best Grandma," pastel flowers proclaimed, stretched across her breasts.

Five minutes later my jeans were sticking to the sweat sliding down the backs of my legs. I hate hot weather. I hate waiting. I hate the thought of dead people that permeates this empty and cramped pseudo grocery store. It saturates every living activity, from going to the hairdressers to the bank. Talk about dying, death, someone that had just died.

I wouldn't listen and I wouldn't go to the funeral. No one would miss me. It'd be packed regardless of whether or not I went, because what does anyone around here have to do but break horses and contemplate death all day long? I looked behind me into the store. I'd have to go back in. My mom didn't have the time to sit and listen anymore. I took her place behind the counter so she could get the bread, cheese, and cold meats tray she had made for the funeral reception.

"Oh, Ah remember when hur an' Ah wur yung tugether and we got all gussied up to go out. Ya know, in those days, well. No self-respectin' gurl wore lipstick. We had da wipe it off before our Mommas saw us." Mrs. McCormic fingered her newly permed hair helmet and took a dainty sip of Diet Coke. The smell of Vicks Vapor rub and White Rain hairspray wafted over the counter.

My mom leaned on the door, tired, waiting for my father to wipe the butchers blood off his hands and find his glasses so they could go to the funeral. She handed him the tray and took some deep breaths, one hand on her chest.

"Ya got allergies, honey?" The World's Best Grandma held her bag on one knee and shuffled its contents. Keys, lighters, the small sound of coins. "My doctor gave me some pills that jest might hulp, shore hulp me with them allergies." My mom nodded the old woman's concern away and smiled at me, coughed into her tissue and said she was fine. My dad put the tray in the car and came back for her. He helped my mom get into their brown sedan and they joined the line of cars making their way to the newly remodeled Baptist church.

I ate a polished green apple. It tasted like plastic. Dead bodies in caskets always seem to me like molded plastic. In fact, that is one of the main reasons I will not go to these affairs, I noted as the thought contaminated my apple and made me throw it into the trash.

I have come to know that every summer at least a handful of the old will die in the demoralizing heat and the entire town will go to their carefully manicured funerals. The young pastor will project caring and sad reassurance by means of a half smile, which he deems appropriate to the situation. The body, neatly groomed and commanding more respect in death than it ever did in life, will validate the entire proceedings.

The newly remodeled church was a source of pride in the town. I wouldn't hear of going anymore. So they left me with the empty store, the diet Cokes, with the Old One who was still talking. "Yur parents are so sweet ta send a card with all our names ta ev'ry funeral," she was saying at me. "So sweet, yur mother is. You look jest like hur." I smiled at her because that was what she wanted me to do.

All day long people wandered in and out, making gossipy talk when they wanted, buying a tub of butter and nail polish, writing checks for three dollars and eighty-two cents until seven o'clock that night when I stepped out and locked the door behind me.

Three kids rode their bikes up beside me.

"Hey!" one shouted, as they gritted to a painful stop, dust making circles around their dirty legs. I think a couple of them live across the street from us.

"Whur's Robert?" You'd think a 300-lb. guy would be really easy to keep track of, (it's not like he blends into the atmosphere) but Robert defies logic. My brother could quite literally be anywhere.

"I don't know, I think he's at the Cowboy Café tonight." They laugh and ride off, the chubby one who loved five-cent bubble gum losing his breath.

I looked across the street at the Cafe. A line of trucks and various bruised cars were parked outside it. Young men stood around them spitting chaw and digging the toes of their boots into the sandy dirt road. Hands on hips or pockets. Heads down, nodding. The small band of mosquito bitten kids pulled their bikes up on the sidewalk in front of the Cafe. They went inside as an old rancher came out, banged the screen door behind them as the rancher lit a cigarette. Old ranchers aren't like any other men. They are forever tall and lanky, with faces etched by the sun, the wind, their long hours and the temperaments of their horses. Eternal cowboys. He stopped to talk to the other men. Nodded his head and looked down, the cigarette hand on his hip, the other on a brown bag of take out. I shuffled toward the Cafe. Nodded to the men in my way.

"Nice evening, is'n it boys?"

"Yes'm," they said to me, shy smiles and nods, all other conversation suspended. They were waiting for me to go into the Cafe and leave them to their cowboy talk. I did.

Robert was not there.

"Hey, girl," Jim Bob called out to me as he joined me at my table, "how come you always readin'?" I shrugged my shoulders and stared at the bulge of tobacco in his cheek.

"Is your name really Jim Bob?"

"Yep, on my birth certificate an' everything. Is your name really Northern?"

"No."

"Why they call you that?"

"The accent."

I sat in silence pretending to read hoping Jim Bob would leave me with my banality. But he never did.

"So waddya readin' there?" he asked, glancing at the title of my paperback. Everyone always wants to know what I am reading. Mostly though, I am not reading. I am just sitting there thinking with a preposterously pretentious book in my hands.

"*The History of Knowledge*," I said, "it's mostly philosophy, really interesting. You might like it."

"Oh," he said with an indulgent smile, "Ah don't have much time for readin' anymore," as if reading was something you eventually grew out of, like wetting the bed.

I got up to go home, and Jim Bob jumped up after me.

"Do ya need a ride home, Northern?"

"No, thanks, Jim Bob. I'll just walk." Hell, I can see my house from the Café. And Jim Bob's truck always smelt of dust and asphalt. He had once told my mother that he thought I was "a real nice girl" and she thought he was "a real nice man" and I thought about going to Chicago.

I shuffled home.

Dad taught me to use the Butcher Boy and the meat saw before they left for Thailand, to grind chuck and weigh all of the meats and cheeses. Unknowing why I was attempting this skilled trade one day in June my mom sat down on one of the stools behind me and said, "Your father is scheduled to go to Bangkok again in August. I want to go too." Ah. And so this was why I was a butcher.

She was looking at me as if it was my line. I looked around me at the empty store and said, "Uhh, yeeess?"

"Do you mind if I go?" she asked, all eyes suddenly, and looking up between her eyelashes, pulling that little girls face she does when she thinks she's taking advantage of you.

"No," I said, "Go, I think that's great. You've never been to Asia. I bet you'll love it,"

"Really?" she said in a small voice, "You'll have to take over the store for a while," her voice got even smaller. "It's just that I don't think I'll ever have the chance again. I found this really great deal on tickets."

She was trying so hard to be cute, biting her lip and giving me puppy eyes with her black bobbed hair and bright pink rouge.

"I'm glad you get to go," I said. "Bring me back a sari and I'll run this tiny piece of hell."

She clapped her hands together once and jumped off the wooden stool to kiss me; bloody apron, hands, and ground chuck. "Ooh," she sighed as she hugged me, "Northern, you stink!"

"I know Mom, I know."

No one was coming to the store, not one person. Thirty minutes went by. I was still sitting on top of the counter next to the register. My dad hated it when I did that. But he wasn't there. He was in Thailand.

"Aaaaaghhh," I slid off the counter and lay on the floor. My legs were twisted and my back arched weird, but it felt good. Ten minutes went by. No one walked in. I never noticed how slow the store business was until I had to be there all day long. This was making me crazy.

I lay moaning on the floor. "Boooored. Booooooored," I moaned. People are distractions, and if you do not have people, you have to distract yourself somehow. So I stayed on the floor. Five minutes went by. Robert didn't look down at me, or even cared that I lay in the same position for however long I wanted to. He was reading a computer game magazine.

The door jangled open.

"Whoa! Waddya doin' on the floor, darlin'?"

I was glassily staring at boots. These boots wore spurs. I'd never seen spurs before. I didn't know people wore them. I started to laugh. I picked myself up off the faded royal blue carpet.

"Sorry," I said.

"Mmm-Hmm," Jim Bob mumbled. "Jest need some sugar, sweetheart. You know whur your Momma keep that?"

"Yup." I showed him where it was. We carried three different brands. He didn't know which one he wanted. He looked at them all...intently. He looked at the prices, the net weight, the brand's names. I think he was comparison-shopping or something. Huh. I didn't give a rat's patoot. Let him have whatever brand of sugar he wanted. I didn't care enough to tell him that the same company owned all three and it was very likely the same sugar in each bag. Jim Bob paid for his sugar.

But he should have been warned by the crazed look in my butchering eye. Instead, he leaned his lanky frame against the meat counter glass and smirked at me in my bloodied apron.

"Whoa," he said with a jolly half-smile to my back, "watch out, she's got a knife. Beware a woman with a knife." Chuckling, I guess he thought that was really clever of him. I turned around, wiping one wet hand on the front of my apron.

"Did you know," I said coldly, pointing at him with that big red knife, "that all but two serial killers are middle aged white men? That most random murders are committed by men? Women don't do things without purpose. If you fear a woman with a knife it's because you've done something you know you shouldn't be doing. Now, we have no problems. This knife is as harmless to you in my hand as it is to me." I smiled at him, wrinkled my nose, and turned back to my work.

What was he thinking? I don't know. Hopefully he was horrified. I looked behind me and Jim Bob was gone.

No one else was in the store.

"What did you tell him?" Robert yelled back at me, "He ran outta here, and didn't even say 'Bye'."

"I dunno. Nothing," I said.

"Yeah, right. You need to stop scaring people, Northern. 'S only funny to you." Robert had a point. It was only funny to me, but I only laughed harder.

And no one was around to hear that either. No one was ever there to see anything I did. No one heard anything I said.

"C'mon! I laugh at you!" I yelled, brandishing a top sirloin at the empty store.

"Stop it," Robert said, "put that thing down and look out for customers, I'm going for a smoke."

"Yeah, yeah. Smoking. Huh. I wanna go out for a smoke." I shuffled up to the front counter.

"You don't smoke," he said, like every other time he went out the door to the green plastic patio set.

"Maybe I should start," I yelled.

I jumped on top of the counter and stared at the broad beefy line that was creased into his neck. Smoke drifted up so lazily that I was getting annoyed. Why wasn't the breeze blowing it away from him? The street in front of our store was empty.

Robert took a drag. Yawned. Scratched the mosquito bite on his upper arm. Stared at the splotchy red mark and rubbed it. No one was at the bank either.

Robert walked back inside.

"It's only noon," he said.

"I know."

Apparently, no on liked the way Robert and I ran the store those weeks. The only thing people wanted it seemed was the stuff I couldn't seem to order right.

"Di'ju know that fur four days, there wern't any milk in yur store?"

My dad looked at me blankly.

"Yeah, I got that ordering thing all wrong. Sorry Dad, guess I'm not the best manager." He walked back into his office and closed the door.

"Forget them," I said to Robert later, "Every one of them. They were lucky we didn't close up the store like we wanted to do.

Let them lay their own eggs and squirt their own milk and then we will see who needs who around here."

Later the same day my parents came home, our lawyer stopped by to talk to Dad. What right had he to look so remorseful? Why should he pity us? He only knew about the store. And that was the part that did not matter.

"I shore am sorry about this, Ted," He had said, shaking my Dad's hand. The lawyer eyeballed me, maybe wondering if I knew.

Of course I knew. The endless funerals, the forced smiles, empty days, those old ladies who brought me homemade fudge, and then the garage sale ("Still too much junk. Let's give it to the Goodwill," my mother said afterwards). And always death surrounding everything, all the time. My dad's contemplative cracking of walnuts on the porch, which he never ate but gave to the dog. My mother's private confessions that the pain in her lungs was great now, and her heart beat heavily. It was inescapable, as heredity must be. Her mother had died this way and she was afraid. She wanted me to reassure her, again and again, how many countless times? She wanted to know; how would I cope? Would I move on? Would my father remarry? She wanted me to convince her of love and duty, honor and justification. To go down those roads with her, take the beautiful memories out of my mind for her as many times as she asked.

"Remember when Robert fell into the pool because he thought he was being attacked by killer bees?" I'd say.

And she would laugh. Tears would fall down her pink rounded cheeks and she would wipe them away with her still healthy hands, the diamond star in her engagement ring bursting into a thousand colors.

There was no escape in this town. The woman at the post office with her watery eyes asked me. The old grandpas from under their battered Stetson's at the Pack-A-Sack asked me. They all looked into our store, or out the Pack-A-Sack, or from their cars, their homes, their public meetings and their eyes would ask me: when would they run us out? My mouth was resilient against what my mind wanted it to say, that I thought they should all go to hell. Yet, stillness sat on me with its suffocating lack of feeling. Full of resignation, every day I went back to the store. That empty, hateful grocery store that was killing both my parents. My father was so thin he began wearing the jeans still too long for me that I had worn at fifteen.

It was already September. It was 7:48 pm. My parents would be home soon from the after-funeral gathering. And I was supposed to be at my first year of college. But I was here in this stink-hole town, with the old retired ranchers, with their illiterate children, and the dust.

I walked to the back of the house to see if Robert was in his room, but he wasn't so I got the laundry out of the dryer myself.

The phone rang but I did not want to pick it up. I took the sink in both hands and looked out the kitchen window at the clothesline. I will not answer the phone, I will not answer the phone, I will not answer the phone.

"Hello?"

"Oh, Northern, it's jest you, is yur brother home?"

"No, I don't know where he is, I don't know when he'll be home." I don't know anything about him.

"Okay, never mind, its jest about the party. Yur goin', right?" What party?

"Uh, I think I told my mom I'd stay home tonight." She never sees me now that she wants to see me, now that I am no child, no passive receiver of her stories. ("My mother died when I was seven. She told me how her lungs hurt. Maybe they hurt her like they hurt me now. My father's new wife made me raise her children," she often told me when I was bad.)

I looked again at the clothesline. It sway slightly in the Texas breeze.

I had not said anything now for at least thirty seconds. Finally the phone said in my disinterested ear, "Can ya tell him to bring some paper cups?"

"Okay."

The clothesline sway. A black Dodge pickup drove noisily by as I heard my parents' Cadillac pull into the driveway. My mother was laughing at something my father had said. I couldn't hear him, but I knew they would walk into the house through the back way, so I wandered into the kitchen to meet them. It had not yet grown dark outside and the orange Lipan sunset blinded me, filling the room. I started folding the laundry. They took a long time to open the door, my mother walking slowly.

"And then she said how old he was, except I don't think he was so old. He was 62, only four years older than you, and you're not old!"

"That's because retirement makes you old; you give up, start driving around in a silly lawn tractor and not bathing," he said, opening the door for her.

"Puddy cat, puddy cat," she said, kissing me and glancing at the folded laundry. "Let's put that pizza in the oven and watch this movie. I haven't seen anything with Humphrey Bogart in years."

"In a minute," I said to her, "you go get comfy on the couch and I'll pop some popcorn. You want a Coke with lots of ice, right?" She nodded and kissed me again, slowly. Everything she did was so slow these days. My eyes must have said so because she put her hand on the olive skin here on my face that is soft despite the lack of her Mary Kay remedies.

"Like a marshmallow," she said, a familiar epitaph.

My dad caught my eye. "I'll be in the office," he said, retreating into his financial world, that fragile, crumbling planet that made him wake up at 5am everyday but Sunday.

They both left me, one for her Chanel N 5 scented bedroom, one for his Beef Today magazines and a Ph.D certified office. I took the sink again in both hands and looked past the sunset. Outside, right outside the kitchen window past the sink and the phone, illness and death, the clothesline sway. I knew it always would. If no one saw it but me, it would still sway. If all the love in one day dried up and left nothing, if my heart stopped when my daughter was seven, and hers when her daughter was seven, it would always sway somewhere. If I could tell all the stories in the world, that clothesline would still sway in the west Texas breeze.

I turned away from the sunset, the clothesline, away from illness and death, from this dusty town and heard Humphrey Bogart over my mother's laughter. I had not seen *Casablanca* in a very long time.

The Painter

Sabas walked out of his studio to answer the phone. "Yes?" He asked, allowing his voice to hang lightly before blowing out an impatient breath.

"Yes, Stan, it's Pastor Reed. Is your sister at home?"

"I believe she's praying or flagellating herself. Hold please," he said politely. He sauntered down the long hallway to his sister's room, knocking just below the 'What Would Jesus Do?' sticker, smelling the floral antiseptic that emanated from behind the cream colored door. He knocked again loudly, because her radio was on, the usual Christian light rock that invaded his studio when the door was open. "Marcie!" he called, "It's for you—his Eminence, the good Pastor Weedy."

The door opened suddenly and he took a step back. Her blue eyes bulged in surprise and he knew—pleasure. She pushed past him trailing the latest in scented moisturizer and shook out her wheat colored hair before picking up the phone. "Hello, Pastor, how wonderful to hear from you!" her voice was screechy, but slightly flat as well. *She had no musicality*, Sabas thought as he went into his studio to light up some incense. Her bad vibes bugged him.

Marcie put down the phone. Pastor Reed's admonition replayed itself in her mind as she struggled to memorize his words: *There is a new Youth Pastor, Marcie. He is quite young and has no wife. I want you, as the head of our God-fearing youth, to make him as comfortable as possible. Hold fast, Marcie. Do as Jesus would, be humble in this role. I know you will show Minister Andrew that this is where God wants him, that he has been led to our small church.*

She was to organize the Welcome Week for Minister Andrew and try to get as many of the seventeen students of the Youth Group to attend. Pastor Reed also suggested she recruit Stan. *Fat chance*, she thought. The Pastor said Minister Andrew was quite an artist and musician in his own right and this possibly would be a good way to get Stan back into the flock. She heard Stan clanging buckets together in his studio across the hall. He spent whole days in there alone with his sinful art.

Often she wondered when she looked at his paintings—tortured figures and obscene colors—if he wasn't an instrument of Satan. But no one else agreed with her. They said the paintings were 'inspired' and her mother had given Stan her old sewing room to use, though he had a perfectly fine room of his own. She had tried asking God for patience with her brother, but it was slow in coming. She had stopped asking for it when Stan changed his name and began burning that stinky incense. There was only so much God could expect her to put up with. She would ask Stan to Welcome week and though she prayed for compassion, didn't really want him to go.

"And God came down. And do you know what He said? He said, He said, come to me, ye little children. *Come to Me.* Did he push them off his knee? Tell them to get a job, a haircut, a life? No. He said: we must be as the little children."

Sabas yawned and Marcie poked him in the ribs. He stretched out his long legs beneath the pew in front of him and folded his arms, checking his watch. *Twenty-minute sermons*, he thought, *were much shorter when there was a Cowboy game on.* On those Sundays, twenty-minute sermons became fifteen-minute sermons, everyone including the pastor anxious not to miss kick-off. Marcie was sitting unnaturally straight, and she stared at the Pastor, memorizing the point of his lesson. Sabas was used to that, but he wondered why occasionally her eyes darted to the row beside her, to where the Y. Groupers sat. The Pastor droned on and Sabas' mind began to wander. He wondered who had chosen the color scheme. Maroon carpet, cream detailed walls, wood panelling, and pastel swirled light fixtures. The pulpit was small, but then again, so was the entire sanctuary. He looked at the Baptismal behind the choir alcove. When he had been only three and Marcie four she had been baptised as he watched from the congregation. They had all been so pleased, one so young dedicating her life to Jesus. But when the fat old Pastor crossed his sisters' arms, clamped down her nose and dipped her backwards into the water he began to cry.

"He ain't hurting her, Stanie," his mother had reassured him. But he knew the truth.

"Dead to the world, alive in Christ," the fat old man had intoned and when his sister did not resurface he only cried harder.

A few years later the fat old man asked Sabas if he would like to follow his sister's example and be baptised in Christ. Sabas had screamed right there in the middle of the Invitation Time. He knew the man had turned his sister in a zombie by killing her and bringing her back. "No, no, nononononononono!" he yelled at the man. His mother had to pull him outside into the outer sanctuary to calm him down. There after he screamed in horror when the service began and so from the age of five until twelve he was allowed to wait in the choir room, watching the man who played the organ.

That's where his love of music began, watching the organist, Mr. Fred, pump the instrument delicately in his stocking feet, touch the keys on two levels with reverence, yes, but also pride. Sabas showed early aptitude and was given piano lessons and later, voice lessons. His rendition of The Lord's Prayer left people wiping their eyes, and made his own hairs rise up. But until he was twelve—"nearly a man, Stanie"—he was told he didn't have to attend the full service. Nice Mrs. Stevenson who always smelled like basil would poke her head in when it was his turn to "display God's gift that had been bestowed upon him" --after many lessons and hours of practice, anyway.

Marcie was writing him a note. He glanced over at her; she was using the Sermon Notes section of her bulletin. "Do you want to come have lunch with us?" It read in her bubbly scrawl. He shook his head and gazed at the pastel covered windows. They were supposed to look like those in a cathedral, but instead reminded him of what medieval men pointed their longbows out of during battle. What were those called? Turrets?

Marcie gritted her teeth and tried again, nudging his lanky torso with another note. "You missed Youth Group this morning. Andrew was very disappointed. He wanted to meet you. Please." She had double underlined 'please' and so he relented. Marcie wasn't so bad, not really. She was a tool to be sure, but he hated the other Y. Groupers worse. It wasn't anything intentional, they were just different animals, he thought. He leaned forward to look past Marcie at the pew across the way to where they all sat together. His mother insisted his family sit as a family, but not so for the other kids.

The girls looked vaguely similar, short or average height, reluctantly modest—sometimes they got away with skirts above the knee or low V necked sweaters. The guys were mostly pimply or smaller than average--he towered over them--and always wore polo shirts or button downs. He especially liked Rick's choice of dull colored clothes, and matching khaki colored pants, pressed.

And then there was Lauren. A nice enough girl who always gave the same answer: "If it's God's will, I will" or "I guess we could all try a little harder, Pastor." Mostly she looked sleepy, picking at her nude stockings. But he liked looking at her. She consistently seemed as if she wanted to be elsewhere and that's what kept him looking.

"And as God's children should we strive, strive, to learn from Him and His teachings. Bow down before our Almighty, extol Him, shout His praises, let Him wrap us in His everlasting arms," intoned the Pastor, leaning his leathery hands on the pulpit tightly, as if to strangle his point to the weary congregation.

How creepy is *this* guy? Sabas thought. He took Marcie's purple glittery gel pen and wrote back: fine, whatever—next to her notes.

The restaurant was crowded. The after church crowd were a loud bunch, some tables full of seven-children families, or other youth groups like theirs. The décor was garish, competing with the noise of the diners.

"And from there to the Ministry," Andrew was explaining to the group. "One day I heard God's call. He told me through prayer and contemplation to work with His young people."

Marcie vigorously nodded; she scooped up her fried chicken strips and crammed them into her mouth. *She probably skipped breakfast to be early enough to introduce herself to the Minister, first thing,* thought Sabas. His veggie burger lay opened, untouched on his plate. No one would notice.

"Is that the small still voice that speaks?" Lauren asked, "The one Pastor Reed talks about?"

"Yes," answered Andrew, "be still and My voice will come to you, Jesus told his disciples."

Marcie kept on nodding as she chewed, her eyes bulging, staring at the Minister. Sabas feared she would choke. He was at the far end of the table, and no one had yet spoken to him. If he continued to sit still-- like a hunter in the woods--no one would. His mother had deemed Sunday School optional and so he did not go. He hardly knew any of them and they weirded him out. Once he came in and sat on the couch in the Youth room only to be ignored by everyone but Lauren who sat next to him and stared.

Sabas only had to look at the new Minster once and know that Andrew had already been warned about him and his volatile position in the congregation. Sabas refused to sing anymore and not even the Pastor could cajole him into doing something for the Worship Music portion of the service anymore. He would happily paint a scene from the more gory sections of the Bible for decoration, but the Pastor had said, "Now son. There is no mistaking God's gift to you in the arts, however, less fire and brimstone and more glory, huh?" And so Sabas had refused that also. His mother said it was a shame and the organist said it was his 'rebellious phase' but he knew they were just waiting for him to change his mind and dance like the little monkey they wanted him to be.

When Sabas got tired of picking at the paint on his fingernails he glanced up at the new Minster. He was much different from the other Y Groupers. Andrew was in his mid-twenties and neither pimply nor short. He wore a collared shirt and black pants, but instead of an insipid grey or navy his shirt was a cranberry red and his slacks hung straight down, not bunched about his ankles like the other guys. Andrew had light green eyes and soft brown hair, nicely cut. He looked confident, self-assured, and at ease. The kids who surrounded him crowded, leaned toward him as if magnetically attracted to that air of confidence, and his expensive clothes and caring smile. They admired him; it was obvious. Marcie was beside herself with joy at his apparent intelligence and zeal. Sabas sniggered to himself.

"So, Stan," Sabas heard Andrew say as him mind began to drift away from the new Minister and back to the quiet sanctuary of his studio. "Stan," Andrew called again over the crying children, the chair scraping, and opened-mouth chomping of the chain restaurant. "I hear you're an artist." Their table got quiet and all seventeen heads swivelled towards him.

Sabas looked at Lauren but she was picking at her pantyhose. He shifted in his seat and put what he hoped was a pleasant smile on his face. "Yes, I paint," he said across the table.

"I'd love to see your work sometime," Andrew smiled, "I like to dabble on canvas too."

Sabas wanted to refuse. No one from church had been allowed since Marcie began her Stan's-work-is-the-work-of-Satan campaign. "I don't think you'll like it," he was about to say but the look on Marcie's face stopped him. *Of course, moron!* He thought. *My sister wants you in our house. She wants to tag you, bag you, and brag about it later.* Her eyes pleaded: Please Stan?

"Yeah, sure. You can come over and see them," he said, still looking at his sister. He grinned and watched her squirm. "They're too big to take out of the house." The group swivelled back to Andrew.

"Excellent," he said, returning to his chicken-fried steak, attacking it with his fork. "How's next Saturday, Stan?" he asked before stuffing the gravy smothered piece into his mouth.

"Great," Sabas said, "And my name is Sabas. Come in the morning. The light's better then."

"Oh I love you, I love you Stan!" Marcie actually hugged him around the waist awkwardly. She fairly skipped to the car. "Andrew has all these great ideas for Youth Group."

"Please don't slam the door."

She buckled her seat belt hurriedly and kept talking. "Soup kitchens, homeless shelters, building houses in Reynosa." She sat back and sighed in excitement. "That's in Mexico, you know." Her eyes shone and she said, "what a blessing."

"You just think he's hot," Sabas said, turning past the Post Office. Marcie was quiet. He wanted her to deny it so they could argue. She loved to argue.

"I'll pray that God changes your heart," she would drawl—just, he knew, to get on his nerves the same way he played Gershwin on the piano to get on hers. "You play that sinner's music to irritate me."

But she didn't say anything now. She looked out the window quietly and pressed her lips together.

As Marcie closed her bedroom door and sat at her desk she wondered again for the millionth time why Stan got to be the beautiful one. He was a boy; he didn't need to be beautiful. She was the one who should've gotten his high butt and perfect skin, his graceful walk, like his feet didn't leave the ground, as if they glided by on air and she hated him for it. Stan was smart and beautiful, funny and sweet when he wanted to be— much less now that they were in Senior High. All the girls had crushes on him—she laughed about that--but he intimidated them. Their confidence was faked, and he knew that because his was real. Stan was much taller than lots of the boys, but wouldn't play basketball with them. Even in Gym when he had to play he did it casually, without much effort or the desire to win.

That had always bugged Marcie. That Stan won or got his way without really caring or trying. He put forth no effort and still got everything. When he refused something or wouldn't participate his mother said he was 'sensitive' and when Stan flicked that perfectly straight hair that hung near his eyes with one crisp movement of his head, she knew. Stan was her cross to bear. God put him in her life to keep her humble and she hated Him for it.

On Saturday the doorbell rang and Marcie shot out of her room. "Careful there, go-getter," Sabas called out and then to himself he said, "wouldn't want to look too anxious."

Marcie didn't even hear him. She knew she only had this one chance to see Andrew before she lost him to her brother. All she had, Marcie knew, was her winning personality and zest for God. Surely Andrew should see that before being lost, as everyone always was, to Stan's more obvious brilliance.

"Hello, Minister Andrew," Marcie greeted him as she took his light jacket. "It's a pleasure to have you."

"The pleasure is mine, dear Marcie." She turned an embarrassing shade of pink, but luckily Stan called out from behind them, "in here, Andrew." Marcie stuffed Andrew's jacket into the hall closet annoyed that Stan could call him Andrew, and instead of a show of disrespect it became a sort of shared confidence. Stan's voice was easy, it implied a familiarity that he just assumed, unasked, unbidden. Marcie went into the kitchen, her anger having replaced her embarrassment. What would Andrew say if she also simply called him Andrew as Stan had done? She reflected, maybe he wouldn't mind. He had, after all called her 'dear Marcie'. Yes, she would call him Andrew.

The studio was warm. He preferred it that way until summer came. Then he would open the windows for the smell of the backyard. But now, the warmness was cosy, inviting, and Sabas was visibly relaxed amid the clutter of buckets, canvas, wood frames, tools, nails, ladders and prints crowding the walls. The studio looked as though a mouse lived there: a huge, packing, splattering, nibbling rodent. Andrew came in and picked his way around the large, sunny room. The walls were hospital white, the floor varnished wood, ruined now—wrappers littered the floor, covered in splattered droplets of a thousand colors. Sabas had no curtains, and beside the reproductions on the walls and assembled art paraphernalia there wasn't anything else.

"Do you sleep here?" Andrew asked when he had finished inspecting the room.

"No," Sabas answered. "My room is upstairs." He leaned over to pick up a flat brush and began to smooth fresh gesso on a canvas. Andrew bent over to look closely at the canvases stacked against the wall beside him. "Representational art doesn't suite you, does it?"

Sabas smiled, slowly at first and then grinned. Andrew may have some idea, but not much. "It does sometimes," he answered and put down the flat brush to show Andrew a few other canvases that were leaning on the far wall—away from the sunlight that streamed in from the large bay windows. "These are my scenes from Dante's *Inferno*."

Andrew's eyebrows shot up—these were tortured figures in Technicolor, writhing painfully on spikes, buried head first into graves, the soles of their feet burned by hoofed devil children. They were explicitly life-like—they fairly jumped off the canvas at him, glowed as if the very canvas was on fire itself. "How did you get these colors? The perspective?" he asked in awe, leaning so far from the paintings he was nearly leaning against Sabas.

"It's a secret recipe. I make the paints myself," he answered, pulling away.

"Incredible."

"It's not that big a deal," Sabas began white washing the canvas with gesso. "A lot of the effect is in the outlining and the background. You see," he gestured to the painting, "the background is sharp but gets hazy the further away you get from the central image."

Andrew nodded, staring at Sabas, fascinated, and watched while he wiped gesso from his fingers onto the top of his jeans. "You must drive the ladies wild," Andrew said suddenly, and though he hadn't meant to, it came out as a joke.

Sabas wrinkled his brow. "No, not really," he chuckled and tugged at his Oxford shirt. "Only 'ladies' interested in the *Inferno* are the Goth types. Not that I mind 'em—I don't. But I can't get on board with that many deep-seated problems, neurosis, chips on the shoulder. I like the other kind of 'ladies'. The ones who wouldn't give me the time of day." He was prepared to go on about the kind of girl he favoured, the pretty, bookish types who liked whatever it was they liked and didn't give a damn if it was uncool, but Andrew had begun to look uncomfortable. Sabas figured that too much talk about the 'ladies' was difficult for a man in his position—a new Minister in charge of hormone raging teenagers—

and a bachelor, no less. How strange was that for him? Sabas wondered; how did Andrew handle the adulation of the boys and the adoration of the girls? Except for Lauren, who didn't seem to notice anything, girls like his sister got weak every time Andrew spoke, surely?

Poor guy, Sabas thought. "I need to clean this off. Could you hand me that bucket there?" he asked Andrew, who had gotten very quiet.

"Of course," he replied, seemingly glad to be given something to do.

"Did the paintings disturb you?" Sabas asked, his back to Andrew.

"No, no. I was just reflecting." Andrew handed Sabas the bucket and stuck his hands into his pockets.

Sabas began swirling the gesso flat brush into the clean water. "A lot of people don't like what I paint—Marcie included."

"Your sister is a sweet girl. I'm sure if you depicted less... horror... she would see the beauty in your figures."

"That's what's really so disturbing, isn't it?" Sabas smiled wistfully, "that even though they're horrifying, they are beautiful. Come on, I've never painted a flabby, ugly sinner in my life. Greek gods, every one," he concluded.

Andrew pulled out an abstract piece from the stack. "I'd almost rather this one," he murmured. "Less temptation and suffering." Andrew laid his hand on Sabas' shoulder. "No, it's all amazing. God has indeed given you a gift."

The visit was over, Sabas could sense as much. He walked Andrew out the door of his studio to where Marcie was waiting for her turn; with the pretence of having finished baking muffins she lured him into the kitchen. Sabas re-covered the paintings—glad Andrew had not asked him where he got his models. His skin pricked with the thought that had Andrew asked, he would have had to tell him the truth: that he used himself for the tortured models, posing in the mirror.

El Don Nacho

H

I.

Her Abuelo held up one finger and mumbled, "He said to me, 'You are a Jew. Never will you inherit our title.'"

Abuelo folded his hands quietly. They came together, his hands, and the ring stamped with the family crest. On the crest were a tree, gnarled and dignified, and a bear straining to reach the branches. Abuelo leaned back, away from her.

"*Te lo juro*, Nineta" he said quietly, a sworn oath, and turned away, still touching the ring.

It was twilight. Outside Abuelo's room, people and things wavered and lost shape. The sidewalk was busy with corncob vendors and their hot pans like iron leaves, with chipmakers and their vats of grease, with stray dogs and stray children. Soft blue light slid on to Abuelo's face through the stiff lace of the far window. The light and sound of people softened his features, blurred the already fading eyes. Dinner was late; soon there would be the tears of the little ones and the squabble of the older ones, Aunts and Uncles talking about their businesses and the meal. But for now, only Nineta and Abuelo shared the twilight between them.

"My Uncle. He burned it. Right before me, my Uncle burned our Title rather than give it to me, the last male of our line. The Title that would have made me a Don, given me our vast lands, our wealth. Legitimacy," his bluish eyes ran tears down into the cracks of his glasses and his face, but he pounded the air with the word: *legitimacy*. Still turned to the window, he wept angrily. "It all went to the State," he lamented, a sixty year old shame, bitter still in his mouth. "Everything but this house," he spat out the word, "Indians. Our land in the pockets of sharecroppers." He turned back to her and held her hand to that soft blue light on his face.

"Ah, Angela, I am so sorry I could not give you more. But now," Abuelo sighed as if she had broken his heart. "There is nothing left."

His hands left hers. The soft pressure of the cool air of the house was like a shape, the stone cooled air of old marble and wood like fingers on her skin. The marzipan sweet he had given her stuck in her throat. She didn't remind him again that she was not her mother, Angela. Her grandfather only told his stories to Angela, never la Nineta, for though twenty, she received sweets, not stories. So she kept silent, and Abuelo continued to weep.

"Memories are hard," Abuelo finally said in the twilight. He was looking for his handkerchief to wipe his eyes, his favourite, a very fine one from a place he wouldn't tell her about. "Do you see those mountains there?"

Outside the window in the weak light, in the distance above the city, a pair of snow covered mountains rose up. One was taller, a fuller mountain in the classic cone shape, another lying flat beside.

"That one is Popo, and beside him is Ixtla," he said. "Popo was a very brave Aztec warrior, who only wanted to serve his king. Off to the War of Flowers, this Popo, he went. There he distinguished himself and came home a hero. Now, Ixtla was the king's daughter and she loved Popo," he looked back out the window, across the four lanes of traffic which had become his street.

"She loved Popo," again he said, his voice mumbled and indistinct.

"And?" she asked, "And, Abuelo?"

But he had broken his own spell and stopped, lost, to scratch the nub of his nose. He stood at the window, suspicious of her. "It is an old Indian tale, ask Lupe. She'd tell you better." Abuelo became stiff and held himself tightly, angled away from the approaching night.

"But you know it too, Abuelo," she said.

"It is an Indian tale, we have nothing to do with them, Nineta. *Sirvientas*, only here to serve." He waved his hand, instructive; "I am only reminded of it because I told it to a child just the other day, to entertain her a few minutes."

"An Indian child?"

He nodded.

"Whose?"

"Lupe's. She brought the little girl to help with the wash." He clasped his hands in front of him, turning the ring. "So many *Indios* keep their children dirty, in *basura* and rags." Pointing to the ceiling he called out, "*Por Dios*, not me! By God, not my servants. I told Lupe when she was in the woman's way, 'Listen, keep your child clean and respectful.' And she has. The child is very clean." Abuelo seemed reluctantly prideful. "Very clean," he repeated, "Thankfully, not too dark. Dinner must be ready," he said, grumpy now. "Where are your Uncles? Never on time to The Dinner, with good watches I bought them, no, they don't use them, never know to use good things."

Still grumbling, the old man left her at the window, calling for her to follow. But she leaned toward the window instead, trying to find the mountain lovers again.

"Nineta!" he called, and she had to give up the search for the mountains and see who would finish the Indian story for her.

II.

"El Don Ignacio," they call him. In his fine suit of another century it isn't hard to imagine this man an important Don. Always his clothes are crisp and proper. The formal handkerchief he offers ladies who sneeze, the dark suspenders that have never known daylight. Down to el Don's socks, he only wears the best. His sons see to it. They grumble over his expensive French cologne, the parts for his old silver razor, the pomade for his hair. Where to buy pomade these days?

Every morning Abuelo dresses in a new silk tie. On go the silver pocket watch and porkpie hat, glasses and shined shoes.

"Hola, Don Ignacio!" they sing out to him on his way to the old bank, an attaché under his frail arm. "Ah, el Don," they call to him as he buys flan for his Nineta. "And a bit of hard candy for the street children," he often says.

"Eh, Don Nachito," he is when Lupe the maid fixes his famous *baccalou* (and later, his infamous bed).

"El Don Nacho," he had been since his boys had grown, disillusioned by their father's stories of grandeur and pockets of small coins.

"What a pity you must struggle, my sons. What has happened to our Mexico? I had a very fine polo horse in the army. Black, sleek, she could prance and bow so gracefully she was the envy of the other officers. But now, we *charros* may only shoot off our guns in parades. So much show, but no sport." El Don shook his head at his two young sons. "Where are your friends, fathers of friends? All Germans! When I was a boy I met Porfirio Diaz in 1928, though he was in exile, through a friend."

And as Ricardo and Daniel grew, so did their fathers stories. "And the parties, my sons. Nothing like those matches of volleyball you say are social. We wore tuxedos and drank champagne." And always, the story of their jealous Uncle. "He hated me, sons. Why? Why. Maybe you will know one day of my burden."

Now men, Ricardo and Daniel could only shake their heads. Tired of stories, each son grew restless, snobbish in his own way. The more el Don stuck to his claims as a rightful don, the more his sons pushed him towards senility and arranged their own marriages to wealthy daughters of lesser names.

"*Si, si*, Don Nacho," they cooed to him, anxious to get him to relinquish his home, his dogs, his gold studded pistols, and the contents of his bank attaché in the interests of his grandchildren. The first son in need was Daniel. "Sara is pregnant," he said, "and without the dogs, your house is so big." Then, Ricardo made to get even, "Vero and I want to buy some land, surely you have stock and assets we could use?" Slowly, between the two sons, the money el Don had managed to keep slipped from his grasp into the cribs and bottles of his grandchildren. Until one day, all el Don Nacho had were his stories and his granddaughter to listen to them. For his sons, el Don had become a useless antique, a reminder that they had once been a great family, and a rejoinder to make themselves as men. They had no use for stories now; the tales had made them into hard men.

III.

"*Prima*!" her cousins screech as she follows Abuelo out to the dining room. The twins jump into her arms. Too big for that now, she thinks. They must be, what, eight?

"How was school?" she asks them as she sets them down, kissing each boys plump cheek, sticky from candy and their mother.

"Fine," Danny says, pulling at his stiff red school tie.

"And Ricky?" she asks, turning to the other twin, but he only shrugs and wrinkles up his button nose, the only family inheritance that had withstood time.

"I hate school, *Prima*," Ricky says.

"You only hate it because you're *burro*, and the teacher puts you out of the room!"

"Danny, don't call your brother a donkey, he isn't *burro*," her Aunt Sara steps between the boys to kiss her oldest. "There, Ricky," she meant to kiss away his hurt, but Nineta knew it was still there. Ricky could not look her in the face and his ears were red. He shot his brother a murderous look, the shame of being taunted in front of his Prima, his eldest cousin, would be repaid.

"Go play, *chavos*," Aunt Sara says, as Danny eyeballs his brother and takes off running.

"*Ay*, those kids," she says, "And speaking of family, where are your Uncle Ricardo and Aunt Vero?" She checks her watch, all pink and rhinestones that still have some shine. Aunt Sarah looks around the dining room worriedly, as if assessing any fault her sister-in-law might find. She leans over Nineta to wipe the bookcases heavy with cheap trinkets and lace doilies, glass figurines and hunting trophies. Above the fireplace is a stuffed bird in the motion of flight. Nineta wonders if it still carries fleas. The room is stuffed with furniture; fat couches and mismatched sofa chairs, tables with tiffany lamps. A plaid loveseat and a sick plant block the front door; the family enters either by Uncle Daniel's dentist office next door or the garage.

"They can't be on time, Nineta," Aunt Sarah says, touching and repositioning the myriad of utensils on the round table. "Did you have a nice little talk with your *Abuelito*?"

Nineta sucks her gums, wrinkling her own button nose, like Ricky.

"He lives in the past," she says, "He still forgets I'm not Angela."

Lupe pushes the dining room door open, holding plates.

"He is very old," Aunt Sarah says, sadly. "And how much he does love your mother!" She takes a stack of plates from Lupe's sturdy brown hands.

Aunt Sara hands Nineta half the plates and goes to the other side of the table. Every setting has a plate, a copper under plate, 2 goblets, 3 forks, 2 spoons, 3 knives, a cloth napkin, and individual salt and peppershakers. The table itself is older than a century and often her toes get stuck in the intricate designs underneath.

"Sometimes he doesn't know where he is or who he is talking to," Aunt Sarah says, and Nineta puts down the first set of plates, careful on the spacing.

"And where is your *cunado*?" Abuelo shuffles in to ask.

"I think I hear the Land Cruiser," Nineta says as the doorbell clangs.

"Humph," Abuelo grunts, facing the door as he opens his arms to Andres' hurried *besos*. Kisses from a 3 year old may soften Abuelo's heart, but aren't enough to ease the rumblings of his belly, it seems.

"Ya, *Papito*," says my Uncle Ricardo, coming in from the driveway to pat away his fathers' grumpiness. "You should eat earlier, you know the dinner is too late for you."

"He tells me," Abuelo grumbles, brushing him off to kiss his daughter-in-law.

"Ah, el Don Nachito is hungry," Aunt Vero holds his hands, "Lupe, bring el Don *algo de comer*," she calls in the direction of the kitchen, kissing Aunt Sara's heavily perfumed cheeks.

"I'll get it."

"No, Nineta. Let Lupe," the Aunts say together, secretly examining each other's outfits and shoes, what her latest jewellery might be, and how much it may have cost.

"No, no, I'll do it." Nineta knows twenty minutes of ritual ceremony will now begin. The Aunts voices will get higher pitched, her Uncles will find each other and compare business news (and sometimes the actual content of their wallets) and her cousins will scream and cry for this, that, and the other thing.

In the kitchen it's quiet. "Mmm," she says out loud, smelling their dinner.

Lupe stands at the stove and stirs the soup, a blended zucchini broth, with an old wooden spoon. Nineta sits down on a low stool relaxing her shoulders. Lupe doesn't look at her, but keeps to her own slow stirring, her head rocking side to side in front of the blue tiles on the grange. Lupe hums, the wooden spoon continuously moving in circles. Nineta puts her bare feet on the stone floor, clean and dulled by so many padded slippers at midnight snack, midmorning eggs, and munching trips to the fridge. Lupe hands the girl a drink for Uncle Ricardo with her free hand. It smells like mint, but Nineta knows it is heavy with Tequila. She licks some of the foam from the top, giving Lupe's back the eye. Lupe knows I want to say something, Nineta thinks, but the maid waits, stirring. Nineta looks down at the floor, the stone sloping slightly towards the door; she is too ashamed of her gringo accent to ask for *pan con frijoles*, bread with beans, for Abuelo.

"Grandfather is hungry," she says.

Lupe turns around to smile at the girl, her eye wrinkles fold back like fans, her gold teeth wink.

"Of course he is," she says, "el Don doesn't eat as he should." Husky and dark is her voice, a minor chord. Her free hand opens the fridge next to her and she pulls out a plate. Nineta takes it and hesitates, a drink in one hand and a bean sandwich in the other. Lupe is still looking at the girl, her Indian eyes two hard pebbles.

"Lupe, do you know the story of Popo and his Princesa?" Nineta asks. Her mother and everyone else would be very angry with her for being familiar with servants, but she likes Lupe.

Lupe smiles at the girl again. "If you come back after the dinner, I tell you this little story."

In the living room Nineta hands Uncle Ricardo his drink, and Abuelo his *pan con frijoles*. With his fingertips, Abuelo spreads out a cloth napkin over his lap, settling down at the table, but close enough to hear the adult bickerings of his sons.

Uncle Ricardo carefully sips his drink, leaning away from his designer shirt. His brother eyeballs the mint tequila and wets his lips. "Where's mine?" he asks.

"Oh, Uncle," she says, "You wouldn't like it, *chavo*. It's got," she lowers her voice to a whisper, "Alcohol."

Uncle Daniel belts out a laugh as the Aunts circle the table; the twins and Andres pulling on their mother's legs, squabbling.

Nineta sits on the edge of the fireplace, next to the piano, and wipes off some hairs and dust from its keyboard cover.

"And I said, *no me digas*, don't tell me she thinks she can go shopping in *Cuidad Mejico* without her *cunada*!"

"We are taking the dogs for the *Competacion Nacionale* in

Queretaro,"

"*Hijole*! *Bueno*, how much does that cost?"

"*Como se va con tu mama*?"

"*Ya*, Mama is fine, *gracias a dios*, but the girl who was helping ran away to Chihuahua."

"*Que desgraciada*!"

"Yes, yes, shameful! What animals people can be."

Uncle Daniel softly kicks her foot. "*Ay*, Nina, do you want to go to Zacapoaxtla this weekend?"

"*Ay*, no, brother," Uncle Ricardo interrupts, "Not with that car of yours, is too small, you know this. Everyone will want to come, your *cunada*, your twins, Sara, el Don Nacho, until you all sit tighter than the poor in their coffins!"

Uncle Daniel clucks his tongue and waves his hand, so much like his father. "*Ni modo*," he says, "And who cares? If la Nineta wants to go, we all go, *ya* Nineta?"

But by now she's confused. Are they definitely going to Zacapoaxtla whatever she says? Has it been argued into stone?

"Nineta," comes Abuelo's soft voice from behind the boys, "They make the most beautiful *textilos*, blankets, and tapestries in Zacapoaxtla. I was there years ago, and still use the blanket on my bed when the nights are cool. And, I will lend you my camera, *hija*."

So, it is decided. The Aunts are still hovering, so Nineta slips in next to Abuelo quickly, before anyone can tell her where to sit.

"Aren't you going to eat?" Aunt Vero exclaims as the kids jump away from the table.

"*Ya*, Aunt Vero," says Danny, "we ate our *fideos* and some *pan y ya*."

"And no *zanahorias* or other vegetables, *mi'jo*?" Aunt Vero hasn't realized yet that she has lost. Lupe brings in our zucchini soup.

"No, no, no," they chant, dashing back into the twins' room.

Nineta picks up her spoon, careful to choose the right one so her mama won't be embarrassed by her. The soup is creamy and light green. It steams, but forms no skin, so she knows it won't make her sick.

"Be careful of what you eat outside your Abuelo's house," her father had warned her. "If you must eat out, never never never sweetheart, eat on the street. No matter how good those carts smell, they are full of bacteria. And, at a hotel or restaurant never eat the fresh fruit or milk. Like me you'll be in the toilet in no time. Regrets, regrets. We just don't have the immunities your mother and her family has."

"Lupe!" Aunt Sara calls out, "the food!"

Abuelo smoothes the napkin on his lap, calm but irritated. She leans towards him to see if he will speak to her, if she can smooth his nerves.

"I asked Lupe to make *Mole Rojo* tonight," he says to her confidentially. "Your Aunts don't like *Mole Rojo*, but I do," he nods slowly, confident that Lupe won't disappoint him.

The smell of *Mole* precedes Lupe by at least 15 seconds. *Mole Rojo* is made from red *chile* that's grown near the city, and chocolate from down south. It's very spicy.

"*Mira*, brother," Uncle Daniel says, his forkful of Red *Mole* stuffed into his moustached mouth with anger and impatience. "I mean, really, look. I have my business here, no problem for money. I fix teeth, I see the old *campesinos*, the people. But we can't afford to go to Queretaro right now. You know this, brother."

Everyone is very quiet as Uncle Ricardo laughs off Daniel's bad mood. "Fine, brother, but the twins want to go watch the dogs compete."

Uncle Daniel purses his lips before ripping a bite off his torta, the bread crumbling on to the tablecloth, and butter dots his cheek. "I think about this, brother."

"Remember my dogs, Daniel?"

"*Si, si*, Papa, I remember those monsters of yours."

"They were very big," el Don says to her, leaning over, speaking into her shoulder, "before the money was gone with our good name." He shrugged his shoulders, pursing his lips. "Life was so different then, Nineta."

"What good is this story, Papa?" Daniel shouts from the other end of the table, "Don't fill her head with such *porquerias*. She will believe nonsense lies like that if we don't set her straight."

"It is not a lie, Daniel. Do not raise your voice to me." Abuelo straightens his back tighter, away from the high intricate back of his chair.

"*Ay*, Papa, Daniel only wants to remind Nineta that the story is very long, and happened a long time ago, it cannot be made simple."

"That is not what he meant, and I will discuss no further of this," el Don says. Dabbing his clean-shaven mouth with dignity, he turns away.

"*Ay!*" Daniel blows out his breath as he wipes his unruly *bigote* free from clinging crumbs. "Nineta," he says to her, an aside as everyone else scrapes gold plated silverware against porcelain plates, "What good is a title if I can't feed my sons? Those days have died; we have prospered from hard work, not the handouts of a dictator or king. Hard work is what I teach my sons. No stories for *mis hijos* of what they are due."

El Don grunts and Nineta sighs, having held her breath so tightly for so long.

"Abuelo Nacho," she says, "if one were to go to Spain, would they find a record of this title?"

Her Aunts and Uncles are silent, staring, food on forks forgotten.

"*Claro*, Nineta. Of course they keep historical records in the National Library surely."

"Even if you found it," Daniel butts in, the *necio* goat that he is, "No one would honor it."

"But at least you would know the truth," she says.

Both Daniel and Ricardo grunt as the Aunts smile at her in sympathy.

"When did the truth ever do us any good?"

IV.

1952

"Pinky, no! Bad dog. *Ay*, Ignacio. This patio is for dogs. It smells of dog, *fuchi*."

"Well, wash it, woman."

"Go to the devil, Ignacio. I will not clean up after dogs."

"Then the patio is theirs, Teresa."

Teresa Magallan Campa suddenly turned and gathered her skirts. "*Si*, the patio is theirs," and with a lift of her head, she glided into the living room. She stopped in front of the street window, its black iron embellishments flaking paint from their artificial flower petals. The living room was in the old style. Large oak furniture reflected the moulding on the ceiling, not so different from the century before. If there had been more furniture; more chez longues, sofas, end tables with attached secretaries, the modest set of rooms would be crowded despite the vaulted ceilings. But they didn't have enough for crowding, and Teresa had the taste and delicacy to carefully space out the Chippendale chairs, the pink French settee to accentuate spaciousness, not bareness. She had left a place for a piano, in front of the window where she now stood, but Ignacio had denied her request. "What do you need that for?" he had asked, "What you need is a damned horse."

"*Venga*, Angelita," she called toward her daughter's room. "Get up now, your father will drive us to the Rovia's."

Ignacio stood and struck his hand against the high wooden patio door. "I will not take you," he declared as she disappeared into Angelita's room. "Mexico City is too far, we are busy at the bank, and," he stopped, realizing he did not need to argue. She was his own wife, after all.

Teresa lifted the toddler from her crib and brought her into the living room. Her face was tired, but set with determination. "Ignacio, I am tired of these rooms, and from this work. I wish to spend some time with my family, and they have not seen much of Angelita." The toddler nestled her head against Teresa's soft bosom, yawning largely, her open mouth clownish against her wide ears. Teresa pushed her fingers against the child's earlobes, re-sticking the tape she had put there to prevent the ears from growing wider.

"There are so many people in this *Vecindad*. I can hear their radios and servants, smell their cooking. I wish for the quiet of my own home."

"The Rovia's home is not yours, woman."

Teresa's eyes flashed. "Neither is this one, do not forget!"

Ignacio stared up at the two-story ceiling, imagining dust on the oak mouldings, and refused to argue. It was true they shared the 16th century mansion with ten other families. Their kitchen was nearly three hundred years old, the pipes and walls rusted and bulged, and the marble of the communal staircase had foot grooves. For showers the *Vecindad* shared the *Casa de Bano Turco*, men on one side, women and children on the other. It was a cheerful bathhouse, the showers were hot and steamy, but Ignacio hated them. To be seen so publicly by his neighbours was entirely disgraceful. Soon, he hoped, the depression would lift and they could have a proper house again, if only for his pride in taking a private shower again, to escape the shame of the old families. The Revolution had nearly destroyed their class. Without guns or horses to defend themselves the new regime dictated they sell their mansions to the government. *Presidente* Diaz had sectioned off their homes, selling them back to their owners in pieces. The presidency hadn't lasted, but the *Vecindades* had. Revolution, depression, world war, depression, all of Mexico was tired of hardship. They were not Indians after all, used to the trials. Give an Indian his *petate* and he was free. Let him lay his mat where he would. But the old families were cultured people, they had no *petates* to lay down.

He stepped toward his wife, stretching out his hand to squeeze her shoulder, careful not to mess her hair or housedress. "*Ya*," he said, "I will take you to the Rovia's, but tomorrow."

"*Bien*," she said, smoothing the child's brow. "Are you awake now, Angelita?" she asked the child.

"*Si*, Mama."

"Good, let's go call next door on Anna Maria for coffee."

Ignacio turned his back on them, regaining his composure. "I must go back to the bank," he said to the doorway. "We are very busy now."

"Yes, goodbye," replied his wife from inside her daughter's wardrobe.

He sat himself down on the settee to replace his wing-tipped shoes and slip his suspenders back over his shoulders. Hoping Teresa would forget the Rovia's, but knowing that she would not, he resolved to not make any plans concerning anything but the bank. Let her make plans and make him agree to them. He wouldn't even fill the gas tank he decided, closing the front door behind him.

Teresa heard the door click shut. Buttoning Angelita's woollen sweater and folding the Peter Pan collar beneath the child's chin, she closed her eyes. The toddler squirmed, anxious to find Pinky the poodle, but Teresa held her down. She could hear Anna Maria Pria's maid singing in a Mayan dialect and smell what the girl was roasting: squash and lamb broth.

"*A wojel ba'axten*," the maid sang loudly.

If she was singing that loudly, Teresa thought, surely Anna Maria Pria could not be at home. Angelita stopped struggling and listened to the song, holding her mother's rough hands. Teresa grimaced, looking at the chapped palms her daughter caressed.

"Carino! What happened to your hands?" Aunt Jenny had asked at the wedding of her middle son. "Does that man not give you a maid?" Aunt Jenny had leaned forward, confidential and alarmed. The party was loud enough to ignore; the women had not seen each other for many months. "That's too much work for you, mi amor," she had whispered.

Teresa had only put a hand on her heart, pursed her lips and stared ahead at the wedding party. "Go play, Angelita," she had said, and the child danced away happily, disappearing into the crowd to watch the violins of the rented orchestra.

Teresa's family, the Magallans, were celebrating late into the night after the festive day. It was a house full of people drinking, dancing, laughing, swirling pastel silk and chiffon. The formality had ended in the church on the main square, surrounded by the huge lush palms that enthralled the children. "Look! That one is so tall I cannot see the top!" The children begged for toys from the vendors; airplanes that flew when you wound the rubber band propeller, bright balloons on strings to bounce against the pavement, miniature cars for a Papa to push as his children rode, squealing. The reception was in a cousin's home, on a cliff that faced the Sea. The house was so tall the rooms were on three levels, and everyone was accommodated in their own room. During the day Teresa could see the incredible blue of the shallow water when she looked out the main salon, but at night the Sea was a blackened hole, pierced by the lights of ships.

"You cannot let that man control you any longer," Aunt Jenny advised her.

"And what am I to do?"

"Well, Carino, if you do not know how to control your own husband, I do not know how to help you." Aunt Jenny studied her best ring, a large pearl surrounded by rubies, as if she had nothing else to say. Teresa turned away, massaging her hands, arraigning the pleats of her elaborate skirt. Then she traced the outlines of the sequenced design- a large parrot in a tree. The sequence was sparse and barely glittered, but the outfit was understated radiance. Ignacio did not like it, but she had insisted.

"How did you control yours, Aunt Jenny?"

"Of course the same way every woman controls, my lovely girl." Aunt Jenny raised her chin. "Though his children."

"*Mama?*" Angelita asked, still wearing only her diaper and the Peter Pan sweater. "We go see Tonio?"

"*Si, mi amor,*" Teresa said quietly, feeling her heart strain weakly.

"Tonio," the child sang, sucking her fingers, unconcerned for the far away look on her mother's face. "Tonio has eyes like sky and hair like sun," Angelita told her mother.

"*Si, mi amor.* He is very beautiful."

"No, mama," the child insisted, misunderstood. "He's a boy, not beautiful." Squirming and still missing her pants, she climbed out of Teresa's grasp and shook her dark curls. "Pinky!" she called to the patio. "Where Pinky?" Her feet slapped the hard tiles of the living room. "Pinky," she cried as the poodle licked the sweet goo from the tape on her ears. "*Ay!*" The child clawed at the tape, pulling out fine hairs until both pieces were gone and the dog could lick her clean.

V.

Anna Maria met her neighbor with a graceful kiss, her fingertips lingering on the child's pale cheeks. They met in Anna's living room, stroking children and speaking in low tones and sat on the divans of the living room, crossed ankles beneath calf length pencil skirts with narrow pleats. She had opened the windows to let in the sounds of Puebla. Cars backfired smoke and fire, cats howled in trash cans, a woman called out, "Ribbons, rubber, and lace for sale!" There was no dust on Anna's furniture; her black lacquered cabinets reflected sunlight from their painted surfaces. The Persian rugs on polished wood floors were clean and the glass of the gilded mirrors was spotless. Teresa breathed a sigh of relaxation whenever she entered Anna's home. She would not be made to do anything for however long she stayed.

"Girl!" Anna Maria called out, "Stop that cat-singing and bring our *cafes*!"

"I heard her earlier and doubted you could tolerate such noise, Anna."

Her friend sighed and brushed Tonio's thin yellow hair aside with perfect fingernails. "She is upset because of some stupidity of my eldest son."

"What stupidity?"

Anna Maria did not speak as Betsyda brought in the *cafes* on white china cups. She watched the maid calmly, pursed her lips and waved the servant out of the room with only a light movement of her hand. "Of course, what else," Anna Maria said when the door had shut. "She thinks he wants her. How ridiculous, a girl like her." She raised her eyebrows and lifted her head high, slightly to the left as if to say, *and it's none of MY business.*

"Mama, what does Alberto want her for?" Tonio asked.

"To make a fool, *mi amor*," his mother answered.

"*Tonta*, stupid girl," agreed Teresa.

"Have you got a girl yet, Tere?" Anna Maria asked as she stirred cinnamon into her dark cafe, giving Tonio a sip.

"Shamefully no, *Amiga*," Teresa put a large hand on her chest. "I think Ignacio is punishing me, the *bruto*."

"For what, *Amiga*?"

Teresa's hand moved in slow circles, "Who knows the ways of men?" she asked.

"Disgraceful," Anna Maria straightened her back, "All that work!"

"He says we have no money for a girl."

"*Mierda*," Anna said with vehemence. "Men are like animals. They have no idea how much work we do for them. Betsyda is *necia*, but I need her. Without someone to help, how could it be done?"

"It is true," said Teresa, "they do not understand."

Anna Maria shook her head and pushed Tonio toward their patio. "Go play with Angelita, *mi amor*."

The children squealed and grabbed hands, clumsily running toward the mid-afternoon sunlight. Anna watched them and lowered her voice.

"I have found a *requerdo* in my husband's sofa at the office."

"What kind of keepsake?"

"The *fulana* kind. Lacy panties."

"*Chingado*!" Teresa hissed, quickly checking to see if the babies had heard. "What will you do?" she whispered.

Anna was quiet, watching the children play in the plants, each trying to find the biggest potato bug. They pinched them off large leaves, screeching when they felt the hairy legs writhing against their sticky palms. Anna smiled, watching her youngest of six boys. She envied Teresa her sweet daughter, that her friend could buy frilly dresses and aprons, patent leather shoes and matching baby dolls. Soon Tonio would not be interested in Anna. He would pull the legs off the bugs, fascinated by pain and power, not the love of his Mama.

"I must confront him." Anna held Teresa's gaze to show she was not afraid, that divine justice was hers. "But I fear he will beat me for it," she leaned back against the divan, hiding tears.

Teresa leaned over to touch Anna's knee. She knew he probably would. "Be with God," she said.

VI.

"I'll wait in the car," Ignacio said the next day, taking off his suit jacket. The wet heat of the capital had made him uncomfortably sticky. On the drive up, once they passed through the lengthy mountains and their leafy shade, the fresh air seemed to evaporate and he knew exactly when they had entered into the city by the water on his skin. Teresa had not seemed to notice, but each time they made the trip from Puebla to Mexico City, Ignacio knew to the precise bend in the road where he would begin to sweat.

"You would wait in this car like a chauffeur rather than step foot inside the home of a friend who is like family to your beloved wife?"

Ignacio nodded only once.

Teresa ground her teeth. "*Necio*," she breathed at him, opening the door of their red Mercedes. Angelita lifted up her arms. "I go too!" she cried, excited to see the big house.

"Of course, *mi amor*," her mother said, giving her husband a big tongue salute. But he did not see her. He was staring straight ahead.

Teresa and Angelita came to the green iron gates of the residence and Teresa pulled the thick braided rope of the bell. A maid in a starched white apron and navy dress came to let them inside.

"Teresita!" called her aunt, "this way, give me a kiss!"

Angelita stood on tiptoe to look through a huge stained glass window behind the circular steps of the atrium to where the voice had called out. The sky was cloudy as if would rain. The sound of high-heeled shoes clicked on the tiles like the sharp tapping of sticks. The little girl looked up at a large chandelier, dripping crystal and dim light, as the woman squeezed and kissed her.

"Come into the sitting room," Aunt Esperanza said, "We'll have our flan and hot chocolate."

"Sit nicely, Angelita, and be careful with your glass," Teresa told her daughter as the maid brought in chocolate drinks, frothy and rich.

They sat on the silk seats of beige and soft yellow, the high backs of the chairs matching the colors of their drinking chocolate and flan. Angelita yawned, the room and her belly warmed by chocolate, milk and women's soft laughter.

"Let us put Angelita in a room to sleep and I will show you the kitchen, Teresa."

"Have you kept the crystal skylight?"

"Of course, and both china cabinets."

"Ah, what a wonderful house, Aunt Esperanza."

The house was a French and Spanish mixture of décor and would have been much more dark had all the doors not been made of glass. Esperanza had also insisted on crystal skylights in most of the important spaces. In the atrium, rooms surrounded two grand staircases that lead upwards to the salon, living room, ballroom and private apartments. The atrium's Moorish arches were high enough to accommodate a horse drawn carriage. During the reign of the French this accommodation was of an all-consuming importance for the old families, desperate to impress their foreign rulers. These days, the large archways and atrium were only truly useful for delivery trucks and the storage of Volkswagens and children's toys.

At times the atriums of old colonial mansions seemed like comedy sketches, servants and adolescents running seen and unseen. They skid across the stone courtyard from room to room, diagonally from kitchen to parlor, servant's quarters to music room, closing doors and whispering what conversations they had overheard.

"Rosa has seen the Senor with his hand on Chicha's backside!"

"I have heard the Senora shout at her for nothing at all in the storage room."

"Does she know of the Senor?"

"She cannot or Chicha would be chucked out of here with her *petate*. She'd be crying all the way back to her village."

"Well I think she is looking heavy. I caught her asleep in the side closet, and have not seen her for days."

"*No me digas!*"

Sometimes when Teresa heard the servant girls giggling in cupboards and behind doors she felt Ignacio was right not to want them in the house.

"Where is Chicha?" She heard a distant door close, footsteps in a back stairway.

"I had to let her go," Esperanza said dismissively. "She had a spare key to Consuelo's armoire and was wearing her clothes on Sundays off."

"*No me digas!*"

Aunt Esperanza pursed her lips and nodded, solemn. "I do not abide thieves in my house. Even though niece Consuelo only visits occasionally, they were her clothes."

"Of course you are right," Teresa said, looking out to the street from the wide salon window.

"How do you like my drapes?" Esperanza fingered the heavy silk and drew it aside to feel the weight. The women examined the texture of the mauve drapes.

"They are wonderful! And such silk, where did you get them made?"

"In Cholula, let me give you the address of the shop. It is here somewhere." Esperanza turned away to search for the key to the secretary when Teresa saw Uncle Paco below striding out the gate. She watched as he leaned on their red Mercedes and knocked on her husband's window.

"Oh, Aunt Esperanza, never mind the address. Did you not mention a new portrait of Visabuelo? I would much like to see it."

"Yes! Oh, and it's beautifully done, come look. I've hung it in the dining room."

"Why do you insult me this way, Ignacio? *Por Dios*, you are even parked on the street." Paco Rovia's voice was firm, but softened by culture and good fortune. He had been waiting for their visit for days now. He heard his wife and Teresa in the kitchen but had not seen Ignacio; he did not understand the reason. Paco had looked around the atrium, the front rooms, and the courtyard before he realized Ignacio had not even stop foot outside his own car. What was the meaning of this? Paco thought, growing angrier with each step out to the street.

Ignacio kept his hands on the chrome steering wheel, refusing Paco a handshake or glance. "No insult is meant, Rovia."

At this Paco frowned. "How can this be, no insult?"

"Teresa would not be dissuaded from a visit and I have brought her. To see the new kitchen she said, or some such thing."

Paco folded his arms against himself and puffed out his chest. "And you sit here like a fool?"

Ignacio grunted. He would not be drawn in. Paco Rovia had been his personal cross since the day he had met the man, on Paco and Esperanza's wedding day. He had a quiet dignity about him. Paco was so tall, a head full of short curly black hair. From sheer size he was noticed, not from any personal or familial merit, but from some enigmatic charm that leaked out of him like so much meal from a broken sack.

"How is your business, Rovia?" Ignacio did not want the lower hand. He had heard at work that Rovia was having trouble exporting out of Spain and that the Civil War was taking much profit from his investors.

Paco knew where Ignacio was headed. The man worked at his bank after all. "Actually, *compadre*," he said with just enough charm to diffuse his sarcasm, "Actually we have just managed to import a great deal of silk."

Ignacio strangled the steering wheel.

"We were helped by an artist. We got him out of Franco's way, *with* his paintings," Paco added, boastful, "and he did us the favor of a few connections." Rovia's mouth opened into a huge smile as he lifted his chin. "We rolled up his canvases into spare parachutes," he said, more for his own pleasure than to incite Ignacio. It was the artist's idea, he recalled, to make his paintings fly and Paco would always remember it as brilliant. He rubbed his curly head thinking of the artist's strange paintings, their explosive colors, and the contained shapes where they should not be. He had never imagined anything like Pablo's version of the world. It filled his eyes, this vision. He would never look at a woman the same way again, that was to be sure! In one of the paintings a woman clutched her heart. Or so said Pablo. It reminded Paco Rovia of Teresa who often did the same.

"You have received my letter?" he asked, reminded of his niece.

"The one forwarded from that quack doctor friend in Texas?"

"The very same one, *compadre*."

The word grated behind Ignacio's eyelids. "Yes, what of it?"

"He recommends surgery."

"He is a quack."

"So you say. Still Ignacio, she needs something."

"She is my wife, I will see to her needs." Why did everyone insist he could not handle his own household?

"Yes of course you will. But if need be she can go to San Antonio with Esperanza to see the doctor. Maybe they can do some shopping together?"

"She does not need a doctor or fancy United States things. She needs to be left alone."

Paco leaned against the car, thinking how silly it was that Ignacio had still not come out from behind the wheel. As if he were awaiting bank robbers to come out shooting to be driven away in a cloud of dust. He was ridiculous, this man, but for the love of his niece Paco continued.

"We have a young girl here who would go live with you and help Teresa with the work. Esperanza says we do not need her."

Ignacio began to wonder if he should go get Teresa himself, or drive away leaving Paco Rovia eating his own bitter good intentions. "I do not like others in my home."

"Surely, Angelita is very active for her Mama."

"Surely, I know what is best for my family, and if you propose one more suggestion about how it is to be managed, I will forbid Teresa to ever come back. Good day," Ignacio said, and rolled up his window, leaving Paco Rovia standing alone in his own driveway.

"Do you remember when they were happy?" Paco asked as he shut the heavy wooden doors behind Teresa late in the afternoon.

"Yes," his wife answered, "but it was a long time ago." The red Mercedes started up its engine and crunched along the driveway.

"Tell me about it," Paco bent down behind her and wrapped his arms around her shoulders. "Tell me when they were happy."

"Once, before you and I knew one another," her voice lifted. He nodded.

"Then?"

"Then," she said, "they loved to sit by the sea in Mazatlan and smoke cigarillos, their toes in the blue, blue sea." She rested against her husband's high hips, leaning back into his chest. "They bathed in the sea before sunrise and during sunset every day."

"Teresa is ill, *mi vida*."

Esperanza knew Paco was right. Her niece was a large woman, and though stylish, and one could see that even the stairs exhausted her. "She breathes with difficulty," Esperanza admitted.

"I tried to speak to the man, but he will not listen to no one."

"Ay, Paco. You stormed in and gave your opinion, yes?"

Paco smiled and hunched his shoulders. "Maybe," and straightened himself, "but I didn't storm. I leaned."

"So graceful is my husband."

VII.

"How old is Lupe's child?" Nineta asked, casually taking a piece of bread.

"We don't talk about that," Uncle Ricardo said, closing his mouth stiffly.

"How old is she?" The aunts were very quiet. They all looked at Ricardo. His hand shook as he wiped his mouth.

"Nineta. We do not," he said quietly, "discuss our servants at dinner."

"She is eight," Abuelo said, as quiet as Ricardo and Nineta could sense his pride.

"Are her eyes green?" she asked him.

"*Chin*gado!" Ricardo banged the table with his fist. "This is a family dinner and I will not hear of this mess over my meal!"

"Calm yourself, my son. She is curious."

"She is uncultured. You do not understand how things are Nineta. No more," he commanded.

"She is my aunt?"

Uncle Ricardo filled his lungs until his eyes bulged. "Say no more." He threw down his napkin, "or leave this table."

Abuelo touched her hand. "Have I told you about my horse?" he asked.

She left the table.

1952

The day was only half finished. Teresa had managed to make the breakfast and lunch meals, clean the floors, send the laundry to the old woman on Miguel Hidalgo Street, and change her clothes before Ignacio returned from the bank.

"It is too warm," he said, rolling up his shirtsleeves to open the windows as the water seller called from the street.

"Agua!" The man's voice was shrill, and he rang a tin bicycle bell.

Teresa had been chasing her daughter. She panted, touching her chest, as Angelita pattered steadily around the living room fighting off the tape her mother was holding. "Nonono," the toddler squealed, holding her fingers against her earlobes, laying them flat. "See, is okay Mama."

Though humored the child tried to convince her the ears had flattened, Teresa was in no laughing mood. Since their return from Mexico City last night she had been hearing rumblings next door. They continued all this morning until now at the midday meal she could hear clear words. Accusatory, threatening words.

"That *fulana*! *Desgraciado*! You disgust me!"

"*Necia*! How dare you speak to me that way."

She was exhausted by her daughter and making the meal, worried endlessly by the shouts and sounds she could now hear building in Anna Maria's apartment. Teresa caught Angelita finally, who was chasing Pinky and wearing her orange organza dress and white apron, and managed to stick her ears flat. Angelita wiggled and squirmed, but then the noise caught her attention. CRACK! Something had been thrown and hit their wall. Angelita cocked her head, confused.

"What that?" she asked. Other things were now hitting the wall. Teresa imagined shoes and bookends making black marks on the wall that separated the two families. They could hear Tonio start to cry.

"How could you? A dirty whore!"

"Will you not stop him?" Teresa lifted her hand in the direction of the sounds, the smacks and thuds; Tonio's cries were growing louder.

Ignacio ate his fideos and steak in peace. "No woman. It is not our affair."

Teresa ground her teeth, picking threads from her blouse violently.

"Mama, what happening?" Angelita was frightened, plaster sprinkled onto her head as the wall shook with objects heavier than shoes and bookends. Pinky tried to lick away the white specks that settled in her hair, but Angelita could not find comfort in the dog when people unseen were shouting.

"Alberto, hold your mother," they heard through the wall.

Teresa shook her husband. "Do you hear that? Her own son is holding her down so that he can hit her better! The shame, the utter barbarity." She wrung her rough hands.

A loud QUAS! More plaster drifted down lazily. Tonio screamed and then was silent. Ignacio cut his steak into small pieces.

"I tell you, it is not my affair."

"He will kill her, Ignacio!"

He sighed, sipped brandy and ignored his wife's pacing. "It is his right," he said, an even tone in his voice. "She is his wife."

Ignacio knew Alonzo Pria was seeing the singer from his restaurant, a woman with *nalgas* out the door. Apparently, Anna Maria had found the singer's underclothes in his sofa. And what? What man did not do as Alonzo had done? What husband can still find pleasure in the woman who bore him six sons? Yes, Anna Maria was beautiful still, her eyes a bright blue, her hair long and fine. But he was not Alonzo. He did not sleep next to her night after night. He did not listen to her body's functions and complaints. Anna Maria was just being *necia*, spoiled because she was born in Spain. She thought she was of a better class of people. As if because of her beauty and birthright her husband was accountable to her. Well, now she knew he was not. Ignacio continued cutting his steak and sipping his brandy.

Teresa had had enough, the tension alone squeezed her heart. But as she went to the door to intervene, Betsyda opened it without knocking.

"Apologies, Senora." The maid had been crying, her face a blotchy mess of salt. "The lady would like to invite you for a cognac." She hiccupped and held the door open, but just enough to slip past as if she did not want herself or the hallway to be seen.

"Yes, of course," Teresa said, though a cognac sounded absurd. In charge of her posture, her voice, and the situation Teresa wrapped her rebozo around herself quickly and pushed the door open. Tonio hung to Betsyda's leg. Abruptly thrust into the light his eyes had grown huge, wet lashes and ragged breath. Teresa saw how tightly the two children clung together and wondered what Betsyda thought of her Alberto now.

"Please," Teresa said to the maid, "take Tonio in to sleep with Angelita. Stay with them yourself."

"*Si, gracias*, Senora," the grateful girl pushed Tonio forward gently into the apartment.

"Do not bother the Senor," Teresa told the girl under her breath, "He does not like others in our home." She turned to watch Betsyda herd both children into Angelita's room before Ignacio could see them from the dining table.

"Teresa!" he called out, "I am not finished my dinner!"

His wife made a fist and touched her chest. "Yes, you are, go to the club," her deep voice carried back into the apartment and Ignacio heard the door click shut.

He looked down at his plate. His steak had gotten cold and slightly white around the edges from the fat Teresa never skimmed from the meat. He put down his silverware and went to the Tropicana.

Squash Blossoms

Or:

Why "Amanda Stanford" Can't Write
Latin American Fiction.

When I was a little girl our family moved from Guadalajara, Mexico to Minnesota, USA. Believing it was of the most absolute importance that my brother and I "pass" in American society, we were forbidden from speaking Spanish, least we end up with Mexican-accented English. Our father was an American who learned to speak Spanish in a California high school, and he was tall and blond and athletic. He had been in Mexico for twelve years before he married and we came along. Our glamorous mother, pink-skinned and raven-haired, read picture books to us in English, but sang and scolded us in Spanish. She had never anticipated leaving Mexico to live abroad, least of all in a place as cold and Scandinavian-flavoured as Minnesota.

I knew we were different, and that I was Mexican. But these were concepts too abstract for a small child's mind, and as I grew, the only thing I knew for sure was that there was two of me, neither of which I was comfortable with. In 1980s Minnesota we were the only children anyone knew with black hair and eyes. I became "Mandie Moody" and fit in well enough, as children are often able to do. In 1986 our father bought a farm in Elk River, Minnesota, with every intention of teaching us about crops, sheep, and responsibility. But he was often away on business, and the duties soon fell heavily on our shoulders and were often simply forgotten. School was easy for me, and life on the farm I found very dull.

In our third year in Elk River my mother threw out some old pumpkins left over from a school Halloween party, and in the spring we found growing, on the edge of our back field, a patch of squash pumpkins. When she saw the squash blossoms blooming, as large as dinner plates, bright orange and thick, she was delighted. "Go bring me some of those flowers," she told me one day, "the ones growing off the pumpkin vines."

I went to the back field and found them, prickly and oozing a sweet, milky sap. Her eyes lit up when I brought them to her and quickly she brought out the mozzarella cheese and flour tortillas. Chopping up the blossoms she rolled them into the tortillas and put them in a pan to fry. "Mmmm," she moaned as she ate the first one, "Try this."

"You want me to eat flowers?" I asked, thinking she was having me on. I shook my head. "I'm not eating flowers."

She shrugged at me, and devoured them alone.

As I grew older, the slight unease I felt did not dispel. My mother told me stories of her ancestors, her parents, and Mexico. But they were always just stories – and strange ones, at that. Then, in 2002, I graduated from the University of North Texas with a bachelor's degree in English literature, and not finding a job, I accepted my uncle's offer to come and live with his family in Puebla, Mexico. After a few months I told him I was taking a vacation and moved further south to Oaxaca City alone.

By January of 2003, the growing world-wide rage against the US's planned invasion of Iraq was at a boiling point. A mob on the *zocalo* erupted; angry and feeling justified, their chanting became shouting, and I sought refuge in a backstreet cafe. The only thing on the menu were crepes, and the chef's special was Squash Blossoms.

I have since lived in many dangerous places, learned new languages, and have my own child. What I discovered in Mexico living on my own helped me write this novel; that while some may "pass", no one can change where they come from – their ancestral history and the accidents which lead to their birth. What I have long known is that much of what we perceive about identity is bestowed upon us by external forces not of our choosing. That while we may, by the facts of the matter, occupy a certain space, we may be forced into one which is, essentially, the wrong one. This becomes the problem of the round peg and the square hole.

This forced occupation of the wrong space continues to happen to me, and has happened to me, my entire life. In 1982, I lost my identity as a Mexican. The loss was not against my will, because I was not aware of having an identity in the first place. I knew I was my parent's child and that we were a certain kind of people. But as I grew, and as I travelled to visit family in Mexico, some of that loss became apparent to me. I didn't know the music, or get any of the jokes, and my aunt once told me that even the way I walked was American – which inexplicably hurt my feelings. At my university in Texas, I discovered that Mexicans born in Texas distrusted my northern American accent; that surely I was snobbishly denying my "Mexicanness" with my tongue's perfect diction – as if it were my choice to have been brought up in Minnesota.

I lost my identity again when I went back to Mexico in 2002. I knew by then I wasn't exactly American, but I realized that being Mexican would be just as impossible. I found the rampant, accepted racism against Mexican Indians deplorable; the government ridiculously corrupt, the society permissive, sexist, and entrenched in a caste system based on a fragile equation of skin color, history, and money. A lot of things my mother did during my childhood made sense to me when I lived in Mexico alone – but an equal number of things offended my half-American sense of equality.

My first novel, *Souvenirs of the Revolution,* grew from these travels, my exploration of my Mexican past, which is, at every turn, violently opposed to my existence. The novel mimics the language of translation from Spanish to English in Part 1 to reflect the historical aspects of the story, but moves to a more naturalized English in the Part 3 to reflect the character of Paulina, who finds, like myself, that she must exist between two cultures – and must move through them fluidly, camouflaged.

I fight against losing my sense of identity every time someone says I'm not "Mexican enough" or that I "must be one of those hyphenated Americans." I exist inside the smallest part of the Latin American Diaspora, so small it is in fact invisible and easy to deny. No one likes to think about someone who is, by definition, both and neither. Like the child who boggled at eating flowers, the woman at the end of writing this novel is unsure if she is being put on – if perhaps, somehow, this hasn't all been some elaborate hoax.

The task of publishing *Souvenirs of the Revolution* has lead me to analyse the dynamic established by "Western" criticism of Latin American fiction (that only authors with Latin American-sounding names may write Latin American literature and no other "Western" genre). "Amanda Stanford" may not publish Mexican historical fiction. To the book-buying world, she is clearly inauthentic, and has no right or credibility in this genre. "Amanda Moody Montes de Oca" is perfectly welcome to publish Latin American fiction, except that she was last seen in 1982. She is a myth, someone who only exists on a passport. She is not I – at least, not anymore.

Come Travel

Get Lost

Acknowledgements

As much as the finished product of our writing doesn't happen in a vacuum, I believe that the nexus – the genesis – most certainly does. It can only exist in the vacuum of the writer's mind, in that still, small space the writer inhibits, and belongs to the writer and no one else.

Nonetheless, there are countless others who bring that centre out from the darkness of the writer's soul to the light. And for help during that painful process, I would like to thank with gratitude:

Ryan Stanford, Maria Moody, Erica Canela, Robert Alan Jamieson, Clare Kane, Liz Michael, Diana York Blaine, Kelly Johnston, Lisa Shapiro, and anyone who ever sat next to me on an airplane.

About the Author

A M Montes de Oca (Dr. Amanda Stanford) was born in Guadalajara, Mexico, in 1980. She earned both her Doctorate and Master's degrees in English Creative Writing from the University of Edinburgh, and her Bachelor's degree in English Literature from the University of North Texas in 2002. She has won two writing awards for short stories; the Keith Wright Prize from the University of Strathclyde, and the Sloan Prize from the University of Edinburgh. Her first novel, *Souvenirs of the Revolution* (2013) is available for purchase in both English and Spanish (*Joyas de la Revolucion*). She has taught English literature and composition in the United States, Mexico, Egypt, and Japan. After spending the past ten years living on four continents and traveling to more than thirty countries she has now settled in Charlotte, NC.

You can find more information at:

AuthorAmandaStanford.wordpress.com

www.ingramcontent.com/pod-product-compliance
Lightning Source LLC
Chambersburg PA
CBHW070334130626
46556CB00007B/2854